"I think we should get married."

"What?" Sophie replied. "Are you crazy?"

"It makes perfect sense," Gregory told her calmly.

"It makes no sense whatsoever. You seem to forget that I've already had one bad marriage."

Gregory flushed darkly. "Why do you assume that ours would be bad?"

"Because it takes more than good sex to make a good marriage."

CATHY WILLIAMS is originally from Trinidad, but has lived in England for a number of years. She currently has a house in Warwickshire, which she shares with her husband, Richard, her three daughters—Charlotte, Olivia and Emma—and their pet cat, Salem. She adores writing romance fiction and would love one of her girls to become a writer, although at the moment she is happy enough if they do their homework and agree not to bicker with one another.

A RELUCTANT WIFE

CATHY WILLIAMS

BACHELOR TYCOONS

HARLEQUIN®

TORONTO • NEW YORK • LONDON
AMSTERDAM • PARIS • SYDNEY • HAMBURG
STOCKHOLM • ATHENS • TOKYO • MILAN • MADRID
PRAGUE • WARSAW • BUDAPEST • AUCKLAND

ISBN 0-373-80595-0

A RELUCTANT WIFE

First North American Publication 2002.

Copyright © 1998 by Cathy Williams.

Visit us at www.eHarlequin.com

Printed in U.S.A.

CHAPTER ONE

'EVERYONE'S talking about him, you know.' Katherine Taylor—curly blonde hair, brown eyes and a mouth that seemed destined to smile at the slightest opportunity—was perched on the corner of the kitchen table, idly picking on a celery stick because this week was Diet Week, as opposed to last week which had been Eat-All-I-Want-Since-All-Diets-Are-Useless-Week and watching with interest while her friend did amazing things with vegetables, a wok and some herbs. 'Rumour has it that he's going to be moving here.'

'So?' Sophie had her back to her friend and she could picture the glint of sheer pleasure at this little titbit of gossip. In a small village, and she didn't think villages got much smaller than theirs, gossip was the oil that made the wheels of daily life turn smoothly.

'So? *So?* Is that *all* you've got to say on the subject?'

'Pretty much.' Sophie drizzled a few herbs onto the concoction in the pan and liberally poured in some cream. Kat might well be dieting, but woe betide anyone who was foolish enough to encourage her in her efforts. She adored food and would have felt hard done by if she had been offered anything remotely calorie controlled when she was supposed to be eating out and having a good time—even if the meal in question was only a home-cooked meal shared between two.

'How can you not be bursting with curiosity?' Katherine asked in an accusing voice, as if Sophie's indifference was a deliberate ploy to sabotage the conversation. '*Everyone's* talking about Gregory Wallace.

5

Annabel and Caroline and all the other Great and Good
have already plotted his entire social life if the rumour
turns out to be true and he *does* move here.'

'Poor man. Anyway, food's up.'

Which diverted the conversation for a few minutes,
but as soon as they were sitting in front of their plates
of pasta and vegetables Katherine returned to the topic
with the relentlessness of someone determined to elicit
a response.

Sophie listened to Kat and her endless speculation, but
she found the whole thing boring. She would be the first
to concede that Gregory Wallace was doing tremendous
things for the village. He had been the man behind the
building of the new housing estate, which, despite all the
initial suspicions, had proved to be tasteful and thoughtfully done, and, of course, all those displaced Londoners
in their new executive commuter style homes would
boost the economy in their little village no end.

Already there was talk of one of the major supermarket chains opening up, which would do away with the
half-hour drive to the nearest one, and the one hotel,
which had been growing sadder and shabbier by the
year, had suddenly seen fit to have a long overdue face-
lift so that it now looked quite elegant, instead of being
the local eyesore. But still. Anyone would think that the
man was a knight in shining armour, charging in on a
white steed to save the poor inhabitants of Ashdown
from rack and ruin, instead of a wealthy businessman
who was simply out to make a bit more money for himself.

'I can't see why the man would want to move here,
of all places,' Sophie finally said, as she placed her knife
and fork on her empty plate and watched indulgently as
her friend spent a few seconds resisting the temptation
of a second helping, then succumbing. 'Those types need

the cut and thrust of living in a big city like London. Don't tell me that he intends to settle down here, plant his own vegetable patch and take up bird-watching in his spare time.'

'You're so cynical, Sophie.' Katherine took a generous sip of wine and eyed her friend with jaundiced familiarity.

'I'm realistic. Gregory Wallace is supposedly an eligible bachelor so why would he choose to live in Ashdown? It's hardly noted for its parade of beauty queens.'

'Don't let Annabel and her lot hear you say that. Besides…' Katherine sat back, cradling the wine glass in her hands and looking at Sophie seriously. 'There's you. You're not exactly a bag lady, are you, Soph? Despite the fact that you spend half your time dressing as though you'd like to look like one.'

Sophie felt colour steal into her cheeks and she hurriedly began to clear away the dishes, stacking them in the sink and then filling the kettle with water.

'Please don't start on this old subject again, Kat.' She hated being reminded of her looks. Everyone seemed to think that good looks could only be a blessing in life, that they opened doors and turned locks and altogether made life a whole lot easier. No one ever seemed to understand that good looks could shut as many doors as they opened, and Sophie was tired of trying to explain that to Katherine.

'Why don't you stop wearing all those long, dreary skirts and baggy jumpers? It's not as though you haven't got the money.'

'No,' Sophie said bitterly, 'it's not as though I haven't. After all, Alan left us more than well provided for.' She turned and faced her friend. 'A guilty conscience can be a very expensive commodity, can't it?'

It still stuck in her throat. Even after five years his name still stuck in her throat and made her want to retch. 'Anyway, I don't want to talk about this.'

'Why not?' Katherine asked bluntly. 'If you can't talk to me about it then who *can* you talk to?'

'I don't *want* to talk about it to anyone, Kat.' Her fists were curled into balls, and she made an effort to unclench them. 'Jade and I are both fine. We're happy. There's no need to dig up the past.' At the mention of her daughter's name Sophie's eyes flicked automatically to the staircase, but she knew that Jade would be sound asleep.

'OK.' Katherine shrugged and watched as Sophie brought two mugs of coffee over to the table and resumed her place. 'But I think you're wrong. You're beautiful, Soph. And I don't mean beautiful with the help of bottles of hair dye and face paint. But you still insist on burying yourself here.'

'You're here. I haven't exactly seen you rushing out to the train station to purchase a one-way ticket to London.'

'Point taken.' She grinned, and Sophie felt herself relax a little.

At least the evening hadn't ended on a sour note. She would have hated to fall out with Katherine. They had been friends since the days of Barbie dolls and pretend teddy-bear picnics but, even so, the subject of Alan was still too raw to be discussed openly, and normally Katherine respected her reticence.

Later, after Katherine had gone and Sophie had checked on her daughter, she stood in her bedroom and thought about what she had said about Alan. All lies. She wasn't *happy*. At least, not in the sense of waking up each morning and being filled with the sheer joy of living.

She only really felt that way when she looked at Jade, but most of the time it was as if she were wrapped up in a blanket of vague unhappiness. Sometimes she could shake it and a waft of joyous air would blow in, like when she had watched Jade's first nativity play at school last Christmas, but pretty soon the blanket would settle back around her body, never quite strangling her but never quite letting go.

How could she explain all that to Katherine? Katherine felt that divorces happened in their millions and that she, Sophie, was lucky at least to have had the dubious privilege of being married to a rich man who had made sure that she was more than generously compensated. How to explain the belittling circumstances behind the divorce? How to explain the way her precious self-esteem had been battered so thoroughly that it had been impossible to revive it?

She turned and in the half-light of the bedroom she looked at herself fully in the mirror to see the face and body which should supposedly have brought her happiness and fulfilment. She saw flaming red hair which curled down to her waist, large, translucent green eyes, a small, straight nose and full lips. She had no need to strip to see the length of her legs, the slightness of her waist, her full bust.

She looked at herself with no affection. If her looks hadn't been quite so dramatic Alan would never have noticed her, and if he had never noticed her then her life might have been different—better. Thank goodness for Jade, she thought, turning away. One good thing had come out of that mire of unpleasantness.

Was it any wonder that the thought of attracting another man, of putting her body on show, filled her with revulsion?

That, at least, was one good thing about living in a

tightly knit, small community. The men were all accounted for. The occasional unrecognised face might pass through, and when Annabel and her cronies descended from London to rest and recuperate in their parents' country houses they invariably brought their chums back with them, but their few party invitations to her had been politely refused. Yes, here she felt safe.

When, a few weeks later, Katherine announced to her that Gregory Wallace was, indeed, moving to Ashdown the information barely made an impact on her. As far as she could see, whether he lived in Ashdown or Timbuktu would make zero difference to her lifestyle.

'And I've met him!' Katherine squealed, over a cup of coffee in the newly opened coffee-shop next to the post office on the high street.

'Good for you,' Sophie said warmly. 'And would you say that you're a better person for the experience?' That provoked a warning glare.

'He's gorgeous.'

'Oh, really, In that case, the locals will probably be eating out of his hand within hours. Annabel and Caroline and the Stennor twins will, no doubt, take up permanent residence here. Where is the gorgeous saviour of our little village going to live?'

'He's bought Ashdown House.'

'*Ashdown House?*' Sophie sat up and frowned. 'I thought that old Mrs Frank was determined never to leave the place?'

'Well, she did. She's relocated to the cottage on the lane, and work begins on the place next week.'

'He must have some powers of persuasion.'

'Absolutely.' Katherine sighed and Sophie shot her an irritated look. 'Along with some very persuasive looks and a bank balance to match. And please don't jump onto your money-isn't-everything soap box. Play your cards right and he might prove to be a hefty benefactor to help your charity.'

'I have no intention of running to a perfect stranger with cap in hand, begging,' Sophie said sharply. Her charity work was a labour of love, and she wasn't about to join the queue of people desperate to meet the wonderful Gregory Mr Fix-it so that they could squeeze something out of him. In fact, she found the whole charade surrounding his arrival faintly disgusting. At the library, where she worked, all the old biddies were full of stories of Gregory Wallace and his no-expense-spared renovations of Ashdown House.

'No, I haven't met the man,' Sophie had repeated on a number of occasions. Now she had to stop herself from yawning whenever his name was mentioned.

She would doubtless bump into him one day. In Ashdown it was impossible not to bump into your fellow residents on a fairly regular basis, and she was pretty certain that she would recognise him, even though sightings, according to Katherine, had been limited over the past few weeks as autumn began to creep into winter and thoughts turned to Christmas, mince pies and Santa Claus.

'Maybe now that the house is finished he's become bored with his little plaything and has decided to switch his allegiances back to London,' Sophie told her, grinning as her friend shook her head and left the library with a theatrical sigh of frustration.

At this hour, nearly five in the afternoon, it was already dark outside and the library was virtually empty. In a minute she would leave to collect Jade from her child-minder, who had her after school on the two full days that Sophie worked, and they might start work on some Christmas decorations.

In a few days' time a large, extravagantly expensive

gift would arrive from Jade's father in New York and in due course it would take up residence under their tree. It was the same routine every year—the present, the thank-you note to the man about whom her daughter never enquired. He had had no part in her life and Jade, only five years old, had not yet started asking questions. That would come later.

Sophie was getting ready to leave, filing away her paperwork into the drawer behind the desk, when she looked up and saw someone standing just inside the door to the library. Because most of the lights in the place had already been switched off, the figure was in shadow and her heart gave a leap of pure fear.

'My hand,' Sophie said in a clear voice, which reverberated around the empty library and had the instant effect of making her feel like a heroine in a third-rate detective movie, 'is on the telephone. If you take one step closer I assure you that I'll phone the police and they'll be here before you can so much as blink an eye.'

Whoever he was, he was tall and powerfully built. His outline told her that much. She could feel her heart thumping madly in her chest and she hoped to heaven that should she have to call the police they would still be there.'

'How dramatic,' the man drawled. He had a deep voice, with enough of a thread of irony running through it to turn it from merely attractive to sexy. He stepped forward out of the shadows and materialised into someone whose looks were so powerful that they bordered on mesmerising—very dark hair, very dark eyes and even encased, as he was, in a trenchcoat, Sophie could see that his body was muscular and graceful.

She recognised the type well. He was very reminiscent of her ex-husband, whose physical appeal and persistent charm had ended up scrambling her brains. She began to put on her coat, and snapped shut the index boxes on the counter.

'Not as dramatic as being descended on by the police,' she said sharply.

'The police? Do you mean the jolly chap who works at the police station and plays Santa Claus in the local pantomime at Christmas?' He gave an amused, deep-throated laugh and continued to stroll towards the desk.

'Who are you? The library is closed. If you're looking for a book you can come back in the morning.' She fetched her bag from under the counter and from habit looked around her to make sure that everything was in order.

'I'm Gregory Wallace,' the man said. She bestowed on him a look of undisguised curiosity for several seconds, then began to head towards the door.

'And I'm on my way out so, if you don't mind, you can either follow me or be locked in here until nine-thirty tomorrow morning.' As she walked past him she caught a whiff of something, some intensely masculine scent, and was struck by how tall he was. It was unusual for her to be faced with a man who wasn't more or less on her eye level.

'I've come for a book,' he said, not following her so that she was obliged to turn and look at him, which she found exasperating—not lease because if she didn't hurry she'd be late, collecting Jade from the child-minder.

'I'd deduced as much,' she said with stiff politeness. 'People who come to libraries are generally looking for books.' So this, she thought, was the man who had succeeded in throwing their calm little village into an excited frenzy. Viewed objectively, she could understand why. He was good-looking, presumably rolling in money and, if the gossip-mongers were to be believed, single.

Look a bit harder, she could have told them, and they would glimpse the trail of broken hearts he had left in his wake.

'And generally,' he said dryly, 'they expect slightly better service. I don't even know your name.'

'I'm Miss Turner,' Sophie told him, without bothering to inject any cordiality into her voice, 'and, as I said, the library's closed.'

Surely you can take a few minutes to locate a book for me. Something on the history of this place.'

'It's too small to have a history. If you want history, try talking to Reverend Davis.' She spun around, fished the key out of her coat pocket and walked briskly towards the door, switching off the remaining lights as she went. She didn't think that he would pursue the conversation if faced with the sobering reality that she might just lock him in, and she was right. What she hadn't expected was to find him next to her and standing so close that his presence seemed claustrophobic. She was not, by nature, a tactile person. She disliked having her personal space infringed on, and automatically she drew back slightly to put distance between them.

'You're the first person I've met who hasn't extended the long arm of welcome,' he said, meeting her eyes and somehow managing to keep them on his face.

'You mean *here* or in life generally?'

'Has anyone ever told you that you look nothing like a librarian?'

'Much as I would love to stand here, chatting aimlessly to you, Mr Wallace, I'm afraid I really must go now.' She stepped outside and slammed the door, turning the key once then testing to make sure that it was locked. Not, she thought, that it was likely to be broken into if the door remained open all night long. Ashdown was low on crime. How could you be a committed thug, she thought, if the person you were mugging had tea with your mum once a week and used to babysit when you were a toddler? Difficult.

She started to walk towards her car, which was parked across the road from the library, and he followed her.

'I guess,' he said, as she slipped her key into the car door and unlocked it, 'you've heard that I've bought Ashdown House?'

'I guess I have,' Sophie agreed, not enlarging on the observation. 'Well, goodbye. Hope you have some success, finding out what you want to know about the place.' She pulled open the car door, slid into the driver's seat, pulled her coat around her so that it didn't get trapped in the car door after she had shut it—which it had an annoying tendency to do—and started the engine.

He rapped against the window, and she irritably rolled it down.

'Can I ask you something?' he enquired, half leaning into the car, and with a shiver of inexplicable alarm she pulled back, her heart beating furiously. Something about her reaction to him unsettled her. She liked men to keep their distance. She purposefully gave off strong signals that she was unavailable, and she expected them to steer a clear course away from her. Gregory Wallace was fast impressing her as a man who had little respect for other people's signals—the sort of man who blithely went precisely where he wanted to go and ignored any protests that might get in his way.

'What?'

'To what do I owe your remarkable show of antagonism?'

'My gene pool,' Sophie told him curtly.

'In other words, you're like this with everyone?'

'In other words, I have to go now so kindly remove yourself from my car.'

He stood back. Immediately she wound the window up, manoeuvred the car out of its parking space and raced towards the child-minder's house. Just before she turned the corner she glanced into her rear-view mirror to see whether he was still there, but he had gone.

She was half an hour late, and when she arrived she found Jade, drawing intently in the lounge, with a stack of paper and crayons around her, happily unaware of her mother's delay.

'How has she been?' she asked Sylvia.

'A doll. As usual. Collected her from school at one, and she was full of it. Louise Dodwell has asked her over to tea on Friday and she's thrilled to bits.'

Sophie smiled, and thanked God for the blessing of this small village where everyone knew her daughter and knew how to cope with her disability. How would she have managed otherwise? Oh, of course, she would have found a way, but it was so much easier to be surrounded by people who knew and understood and accommodated.

She approached Jade and spent a few seconds breathing in her presence, quietly treasuring the miniature copy of herself. It was a shame, she often thought, that her parents were not alive to see Jade. Then she walked directly in front of her daughter, stopped and spoke clearly and slowly, using hand movements as necessary to ask her how her day had been. She received a series of hand movements in response.

'She's not handicapped,' the specialist had patiently told her years ago, when Sophie had first noticed that her daughter didn't seem to respond to sounds the way she should have. 'She's deaf. Not profoundly. She *can* hear, but sounds are a distant rumble and make no sense to her. But deafness isn't life-threatening, Sophie. You'll need to take time, but you'll be surprised at how well Jade will cope with her disability.'

Everyone in the village knew that Jade was deaf, and because all the children had grown up with the knowledge they always made sure that they were standing in front of her when they spoke. They were curiously gentle with her and from day one at school Jessie, Jade's teacher, had learnt basic hand movements and had taught them to her class, turning the lesson into fun so that gradually the children began to mix their words with movements.

Sophie herself had read everything there had been to read on the subject from the time the diagnosis had been confirmed. She had taught herself how to talk, using her hands, and she had started fund-raising in Ashdown and further afield, money that would go to national children's charities. All the time she was also relentlessly reliving the despair of her broken marriage.

In time, she had stopped thinking that Jade's deafness was some sort of obscure punishment for being a failure at holding her marriage together, but thoughts of Alan still left a taste of bitterness in her mouth.

She tried not to think of him, but she knew that she would never again trust a man, never again open herself up to be hurt. In the space of five years she had grown up and shed her youthful vulnerabilities, like a snake that has shed its outer skin.

That made it all the more infuriating to find, as she lay in bed that night, that at the back of her mind there were suddenly images of Gregory Wallace, which flitted about like mosquitoes on a hot night, buzzing in the darkness, waiting to feed.

Hopefully, she wouldn't lay eyes on him again or, at least, if she did it would be only in passing and from the opposite side of a street. She could always avert her eyes and pretend that she hadn't seen him. It would be difficult since he stood out in Ashdown like a Martian at a tea party but not totally impossible. Really, he would be around very little. Tycoons had no part in village life. Their bases were always in London and the country house was the status symbol they escaped to once a month if they could spare the time.

When, the following day, she looked up at a little before twelve and saw him approaching her at the counter in the library she wasn't sure if she was surprised or taken aback. Or both. She just knew that her stomach began to do weird somersaults and the counter, behind which she had been snugly cocooned, now felt like a cage from which rapid escape would be a problem.

In the cold light of day he was even more alarming than he had appeared the evening before. She could now see his face clearly—the harshly chiselled features, the intense darkness of his eyes, the aggressive line of his jaw. He walked with the confidence of a jungle animal, prowling its patch, and stopped on the way to her desk to say something to one of the people in the library.

For someone who had only just arrived on the scene he certainly had established himself, Sophie thought cynically. She assumed it was all that charm and good looks. Alan had had a similar effect on people. He had lived his life creating an outward impression, delighting in the adulation of people who only saw the smooth, easy charm and were ignorant of what lay beneath it.

She looked at him critically as he neared the desk, and remained silent as he finally arrived and stood on the opposite side of the counter.

'I'm back,' he said, as though she couldn't see that for herself.

'So I see.'

'And has this bright, freezing day improved your temper?' He looked at her, and even though he was only looking at her face Sophie had the unnerving impression that he was also taking in everything else about her—her body, her clothes, the way she was standing.

He couldn't fail to be disappointed if what he'd had in mind had been a bemused country bumpkin eligible for chatting up. Her skirt was long, almost down to her ankles, in sobering black and grey, her tights were thick and her jumper revealed absolutely nothing of what lay underneath it. She had tied her hair back into a long, French plait and was wearing so little make-up that she might well have not bothered.

'I take it that you've returned for your book on the wildly exciting history of Ashdown?' She pointed to a section of the library just behind her and to the left. 'You might find something there.'

'Care to show me?' He wasn't smiling but she got the feeling that somewhere inside he was. Cool, urbane, amused by someone, she supposed, whom he considered quaintly lacking in social graces.

'I'm afraid I can't leave my post. I can get Claire to show you.'

'You're right. You can hardly wriggle out of your box for five minutes just in case there's a stampede of people, wanting to take books out.'

'That's right,' Sophie said coolly, not bothering to rise to the bait. She knew that she was being ungracious but she had unpleasant memories of men of his ilk, and if he didn't care for her attitude then that was tough.

'Why don't we get Claire to man your post? Where is she?'

'Oh, all right,' Sophie told him. She lifted the flap of the counter and slipped out. 'If you'd care to follow me?' she said, glancing at him over her shoulder. Before he could reply she headed towards the local section of the library, stopping in front of the one shelf, which she pointed out to him.

'I'm afraid that's it,' she said. 'Your best bet is…this one.' She flicked out a wafer-thin book, which she handed to him, and he obediently looked at it, turning it over in his hands.

'Fine.' He smiled at her and she grimaced politely in return.

'Like I told you yesterday, Mr Wallace, if you want any detailed information it's probably a good idea to chat to a few of the local residents.' Not, she thought, that you probably haven't already. Judging from what she had heard thus far, he was well on his way to having a bigger social life than she had, and she had been born and bred in Ashdown.

'What about you?' he asked, when she was safely back behind the counter and dealing with his membership of the library.

'What about me?' Sophie asked, looking up vaguely at him.

'Why,' he continued patiently, 'don't you have lunch with me now and you can tell me all about your charming little village?'

'Sorry,' Sophie said immediately, 'I can't.'

'Why not?'

'Because I work through lunch.'

He looked around him, as though mystified by that statement. 'Why?'

'Because…because…' She sighed heavily and folded her arms. The library was hardly the centre of a buzzing metropolis. Right now there were five people there, if you discounted a handful of pre-school children who were regulars at the library and were generally accompanied by their harassed mothers.

Usually Sophie took over when they came, reading books to the kids and teaching them the rudiments of the alphabet. She enjoyed it and it left their mums time to choose books without the stress of their children in their wake. But none of this necessitated working through lunch, she thought, following his train of thought.

'Because,' she said, 'I just do.' When he continued to look at her without comment she said irritably, 'Well, all right. I don't *work* through lunch, but I stay here and eat my sandwich and read.' She threw him a challenging look, which appeared not to rattle him in the slightest.

'Anyway,' she carried on, 'I'm surprised that you have time to have lunch here. Shouldn't you be at your office in London? Working all the hours under the sun? Building your empires?'

'Everyone needs a break from empire-building,' he said, and the corners of his mouth twitched as though he was holding back a hearty laugh.

'I didn't think I'd said anything funny, Mr Wallace.'

'Please stop calling me Mr Wallace. Not even my bank manager calls me that.'

Probably, she thought, because he wants to bend over backwards to be chummy just in case you decide to take your valuable business elsewhere. Alan had had a similar effect on people. They had always pandered to his need to be admired. Instinctively she scowled, remembering her naïveté at the beginning of their relationship when her head had been somewhere in the clouds and she had thought that her personality had drawn him to her.

Before she'd realised that all he'd wanted had been something strikingly ornamental to have draped on his arm. It made her hair curl now to think of how she had been so malleable. She had allowed him to dress her precisely as he had wanted—in dresses that she had found too revealing and shoes which had made her feel like a giant next to most of the other women with whom she had come into contact.

'I've lost you,' Gregory said, leaning against the counter with one hand tucked into his trouser pocket.

'What?' Sophie returned from her pilgrimage into the past and refocused on the man standing in front of her. She wished obscurely that she had never come into contact with him, then she reminded herself that she was being foolish because she hardly knew him and it was impossible for a complete stranger to have any sort of impact on her carefully regulated life. Still, it would help if he didn't exude quite such powerful charisma.

'You were a million miles away just then.'

'Here you are.' She ignored his remark and handed him his membership card, which he took and tucked away in his wallet.

'So, now we've established that you needn't stay here for lunch, will you accept my invitation?'

She heard the magnetic, charming persuasiveness in his voice with a vague sensation of terror.

'No.'

He shook his head and gave her an impatient, perplexed look.

'When do I need to get this book back to you?' he asked, straightening and standing back from the counter.

'Within two weeks or else I'm afraid I'll have to apply a fine.'

'Which is?'

'I can't remember. Everyone returns their books long before they become overdue.'

'How virtuous of them.'

'It's a virtuous community,' Sophie said politely, and he raised his eyebrows expressively.

'Really...' he said softly. 'Yourself included?'

She could feel the colour rush into her face and she fought back an instinctive urge to slap his face. He hadn't said anything rude or insulting, but the mere fact that he had made her blush with embarrassment, which was something she hadn't done for longer than she cared to remember, made her hackles rise.

'Especially myself,' she said, meeting his gaze without blinking. 'You might want to remember that.' After a few seconds of silence she turned away and began to return books to their respective shelves.

CHAPTER TWO

FOUR days later Sophie decided to see for herself what was happening at Ashdown House.

She told herself that his was because she seemed to hear nothing but second-hand reports of massive reconstruction, and curiosity had finally got the better of her. Besides, she reasoned, she had a free day, with Jade at school and no work at the library. Despite the fact that it was bitterly cold, it was also temptingly sunny—too sunny to stay indoors, doing housework.

More to the point, Gregory Wallace was safely ensconced in London, according to Kat who seemed to know details of the man's movements with remarkable intimacy. That was nothing unusual in Ashdown. There was no such thing as a secret life in the village. The smallness of the place made any such thing a complete impossibility.

As soon as she had returned to her cottage, having dropped Jade off at school, she hopped onto her bicycle. She'd made sure that she was securely wrapped up in as many layers of clothing as was humanly possible, without restricting movement, and headed off in the direction of the house.

The place wasn't far from the village, but set right back from the road and picturesquely positioned on the sloping crest of a hill so that it commanded views in all directions.

In its heyday, before Sophie's time, it had been the focal point of the village. Angela Frank had lived there with her son and her husband, and had entertained in

24

grand style. Beautiful young things had gathered on the rolling lawns in summer, lazily sipping champagne and dressed to the nines. There had been croquet parties, which had started at lunchtime and supposedly meandered with ever more raucousness well into the late hours of the night. They were all second-hand and third-hand stories, which Sophie swallowed with a hefty pinch of salt since memories were usually unreliable when it came to accuracy.

All she knew for certain was that on the day Angela Frank's husband and son were killed in a car crash the glamorous life at Ashdown House had come to a grinding halt. That had been over three decades ago, and until the place had been sold old Mrs Franks had lived there, surrounded by memories, with the house pitifully neglected and falling into a gradual state of disrepair.

Until now, Sophie thought as she cycled towards the house. The breeze whipped her hair around her face and promised at least two hours of hard labour to get the tangles out, and her hands, in their black fingerless gloves, gripped the handlebars of the bike. Until Gregory Wallace, that knight in shining armour, had descended on their village, kick-started it into a hum of activity and now, presumably, saw himself poised to become the lord of the manor.

At that thought she instinctively gave a little frown of distaste, and was still frowning when she finally arrived at the house, cutting through the back way so that she emerged facing the rear of the house, with a forested patch behind her and the fields stretching down towards the road.

She could hear the sounds of work in progress, drifting on the air towards her from the front of the house, but rather than head in that direction she climbed off her bike and left it lying on the grass. She began to stroll along the rear façade, peering into windows. Things were definitely happening inside. The carpets had all been ripped up and through some of the open doors she could see more signs of things happening.

As they would be, she thought to herself, when the man in question was rich, powerful and involved in the construction business. He probably, she thought as she peered into a room but found it difficult to make out anything because timber boards were leaning against the windows, just had to snap his fingers and an entire design team would appear in front of him. Willing, able and, of course, committed to putting his little pet project ahead of whatever else they had on their calendar. Because, frankly, he owned them.

He might come across as Mr Charm personified, but she knew enough about his type to know that any such charm was just a façade for the single-minded ruthlessness of the born opportunist. He would laugh and be warmly humorous to the outside world, but when he closed his doors and the mask slipped he would simply be another man whose only goal in life was to trample over those closest to him in order to remain at the top of his personal pecking order.

She wrapped her arms around herself, feeling the breeze cut through her clothes to settle its teeth on her flesh, and peered into another room, where three men were working with impressive efficiency. Walls were being plastered and there were rolls of wallpaper in one corner of the room. She squinted and tried to decipher the pattern, but failed.

Katherine had not been lying when she'd said that the place was undergoing a major overhaul.

She stretched forward, avoiding the shrubbery underneath the window, and was leaning against the windowsill, with her body supported by her hands, when a voice said from behind her, 'Enjoying yourself?'

The shock of being addressed when she'd believed herself to be unobserved almost made her fall forward into the shrubbery. Instead, she propelled herself backwards and spun around to be confronted by Gregory who was standing, looking at her, with his arms folded and an aggravating look of amusement on his face.

'What are *you* doing here?' Sophie said, highly flustered at being caught red-handed doing something she would not have dreamt of doing under normal circumstances. Namely, snooping.

'What am *I* doing here?' He appeared to give the question a great deal of thought, then his brow cleared and he said, as though bowled over by a sudden revelation. 'Oh, yes, I remember. I live here!'

A sudden gust of wind blew Sophie's hair across her face, and she pushed it aside, tucking it irritatedly behind her ear. 'I was told that you were going to be in London.'

'Aren't gossips unreliable?' He stared at her as her face became redder, then rescued her from complete humiliation by saying lazily, 'Actually, I *was* supposed to be in London until tomorrow, but I rescheduled my meeting so that I could come up here and see what was happening to the work on the house.' He was, she saw, still dressed in a suit of charcoal grey, visible beneath his coat, which seemed to add height and width to him so that he appeared even more daunting than she remembered.

'I apologise if I was trespassing on your land,' Sophie said stiffly, glancing around and making sure that her bike was where she had left it.

'But you happened to be in the general vicinity...?'

'No.'

'Ah, in that case, you must mean that you made a special trip out here just to see what was going on.'

'That's right.' Now that she wasn't moving it was much colder than she had thought. Bitterly cold, in fact.

'I didn't see a car out front.'

'I came on my bike.' She nodded briefly in the direction of the abandoned bicycle and fought down the urge to sprint over to it, jump on and cycle away from the house as fast as she could pedal.

'Cold out here.' He looked around him, enjoying, she thought sourly, every moment of her discomfort. The breeze obligingly picked up, gusting through the empty branches of the trees and making the shrubbery rattle against the side of the house. 'Why don't you come inside? Then you can see exactly what I'm doing to the place and you can put your curiosity to rest.'

'I'm not that curious, thank you.'

'Oh, for heaven's sake. What *is* your problem?'

'I don't *have* a problem, and it's too cold to stand around here, arguing the point. If you'll excuse me, I'll just hop on—'

'Don't be so bloody ridiculous,' he cut in impatiently. 'Everyone's curious about what I'm doing to the place. It's only natural, and if you can't admit that you are as well then you're a damned hypocrite.'

Sophie's mouth fell open. 'Just who do you think you are?' she finally demanded, in a high voice.

'The owner of this property and someone who is fairly intolerant of stupidly stubborn women who are afraid of saying what they're thinking.'

Sophie looked at him, speechless. 'You may see fit, Mr Wallace, to address the women in your life like that, but let me tell you—'

'Oh, for God's sake. This is the second time I've ever met you and I'm fast beginning to think that you are the most infuriating woman on the face of the earth. Now why don't you just climb down off your high horse, escape the wind out here for a minute and come inside. You're quite safe with me. There are dozens of workmen in the house.' He glanced at her and his look was enough to tell her that even if his house had been completely empty of all signs of life she would still have been eminently safe with him.

She had no reason to even remotely doubt his word. She knew what she looked like. More than that, she revelled in what she looked like. Her face was bare of all make-up, her hair a mass of curls and knots, her curves well shielded in a long skirt, woollen tights, ankle-length, lace-up boots and two baggy jumpers under which nestled, even less erotically, a thermal vest and a T-shirt. The fingerless gloves were the final touch.

'If it's not too much trouble,' Sophie said, because refusing now seemed childish.

'If it was too much trouble,' he said, leaning slightly towards her, 'I wouldn't have asked, would I?'

Sophie shrugged and looked away towards the gardens, wondering whether he had any plans for those as well. Perhaps a few fountains here and there, the odd statue sticking out from behind some plants. Who knew what the man's tastes were?

She would be interested in seeing what he was doing to the house, though. She had been inside several times and had always been vaguely depressed at the gradual decline.

Wouldn't Kat give her eye teeth for this? she thought with a sudden smile. Personal escort by the Big Man himself.

'You're smiling,' Gregory said from next to her, and she suddenly realised that he had been observing her, which made her feel like a bug under a microscope. 'I wondered whether you could.'

'What exactly is that supposed to mean, Mr Wallace?'

'Do you think we might dispense with the formalities?' They began to walk around the side of the house, where builders were working in a manner never before seen by Sophie. Quite a few were local men, and she recognised them and nodded. One she stopped and spoke to.

'James, can I ask how come you never seemed to work this hard for me when you were doing my kitchen?' She smiled broadly and secured her hair with her hand. He was her age, married with four children and had gone to school with her a lifetime ago.

'You would keep offering me cups of tea. Earl Grey is a killer on my concentration.' They laughed.

'How's Claire and the children?'

'Have four kids and you won't need to ask that question.' That made them laugh again.

'You were lying about that gene pool,' Gregory said, as they moved into the house.

'What are you talking about now?'

'You *can* relax. Which means it must just be me.' He stood in the doorway and looked around him, his sharp eyes missing nothing.

Sophie ignored his remark. Ignored him, in fact, and began to walk around the hall, amazed at how much had been accomplished in a short space of time. The dingy carpets had all been ripped up, and black and white tiles had been laid, which opened up the hall. A new banister of oak was in the process of being constructed, and the walls were being primed for wallpaper.

'I'll show you around,' he said, taking her by her elbow. She politely but pointedly removed his hand.

'I'm not going to molest you,' he grated, with an ill-humoured frown.

'I never implied that you were,' Sophie said coolly, looking at him and not blinking, 'but I would still rather that you kept your hands to your sides.'

He muttered something under his breath, which she pretended not to hear, and began to show her around the bits of the house which had already been done.

It was a sprawling Victorian mansion. Her own cottage could have fitted several times into the downstairs alone. Everything was tasteful and immaculately done. Three of the rooms were already complete and the rest were fast on their way to getting there.

'It's rather a large house for one person, wouldn't you say?' she asked, as they strolled into the sitting room, which was now virtually unrecognisable from the fairly dilapidated affair it had been previously. She recognised several pieces of furniture, which he had clearly bought from Mrs Franks because, doubtless, they would have been too cumbersome to find a home for in her new premises.

'Unless,' she continued, walking around the room and reluctantly liking what she saw, 'you're very ambitious about having hordes of children.'

'Oh, I think a dozen or so should do the trick.' He looked at her, his eyebrows raised. 'Does that come under the category of being ambitious about having children?'

'No, it comes under the category of outright lie.'

He laughed and continued to watch her, which didn't disturb her in the slightest. Let him watch as much as he liked, just as long as he didn't touch. She didn't feel threatened anyway because she knew that he was watching her with frank curiosity, and she suspected that that was because she so snugly fitted his idea of what a country girl would look like. He probably thought that things like make-up and fashionable clothes were difficult to get hold of so far out of London. No doubt he would change his mind when he met Ashdown's semi-resident in-crowd. Much more his cup of tea.

'Well,' she said, when they were back in the tiled hall, 'thank you very much for the tour of your house. It's very nicely done.'

'Why don't you have a cup of tea before you leave?' he said by way of an answer. 'The kitchen is fully operational, as you'd expect with builders in the house.'

'They do generally like their cups of tea, don't they?' Sophie said politely. She looked at her watch, shook her head and said that she had to go.

'Where?'

'What do you mean—where?' The nerve of the man was beyond compare, she thought. Was it any of his business where she was going?'

'To the library?'

'No, as a matter of fact.' Not that it's any of your concern, her voice implied. When he remained, with his head slightly cocked, as though awaiting more on the subject, she said, clicking her tongue, 'I have a lot of housework to do.'

'Housework that can't wait for half an hour?' He began to stroll in the direction of the kitchen and, much to her annoyance, she found herself following. By the time she got there it seemed pointless to spend ten minutes pursuing the argument so she reluctantly took a seat at the kitchen table and waited while he made them a mug of tea.

'Where do you live?' he asked, sitting opposite her. He had removed his coat, but he still looked incongruous in the half-finished kitchen with his expensive suit. The units had been ripped out, as yet to be replaced, but there

was a new Aga where the old one had been and, of
course, the counter on which the kettle sat was littered
with the evidence of builders in residence—mugs, sugar,
a jumbo-sized bottle of instant coffee, an even more
jumbo-sized box of teabags and two bottles of milk, both
of which appeared to be on the go.

'Within cycling distance of here,' Sophie answered.
'As does nearly everyone in the village.'

'How long have you lived here?'

'A long time.' She sipped from the mug, cradling it
in her hands, and hoped that he didn't intend to pursue
a personal line of conversation because she would soon
have to steer him off firmly. He might not be interested
in her as a woman, but any interest was unwelcome. She
wasn't in the business of dispensing confidences about
her private life.

'That tells me a lot.'

She didn't answer. 'You don't intend to live here full
time, do you?' she asked, making no attempt to apologise for her abruptness.

'It's an idea,' he said casually, 'Why? Don't you consider it a good one?'

Sophie shrugged. 'Well, you can do as you please but,
frankly, I don't think this village is suited to a person
like you.' Which, she thought immediately, had come
out sounding far ruder than she'd intended. She could
see from the expression on his face that he was less than
impressed with the remark.

Why beat around the bush, though? Men like Gregory
Wallace—men like Alan—lived in the fast lane. She had
brought Alan to Ashdown precisely three times and he
had hated it.

'Like living in a morgue,' he had said. Lying in bed
next to him, still invigorated with the newness of
London, the newness of her job there, the newness of

the man about whom she had initially been wary but who had eventually swept her off her feet, she had pushed aside the uneasiness she had felt, hearing him say that.

Apart from three years at university and six months in London, she had lived in Ashdown all her life and she had loved it. It was small but, then, so was she. If he hated Ashdown what did he think of her? Really? It had only been later she had discovered that, and by then she was already Mrs Breakwell.

'A person like me?' he asked coldly.

'Oh, sorry,' she said, finishing her tea and standing up. 'I didn't mean to sound rude.'

'But…?' He didn't stand up and when their eyes met she could see that all traces of amusement had vanished. She caught a glimpse of the man who had built an empire, who was worth millions. She wondered, fleetingly, how many women he had bowled over, how many women had responded to that air of ruthlessness which lay so close to that charming exterior. Even though she was immune to that combination, she wasn't an idiot. She could see the attraction there, as glaringly obvious as a beacon on a foggy night.

'But,' she said, slinging her bag temporarily on the kitchen counter so that she could give him the benefit of a reply, 'you strike me as the sort of man who lives hard and plays hard. Ashdown isn't the sort of place where either gets done. Life here is conducted at an easy pace, Mr Wallace—Gregory. No clubs, no fancy restaurants, no theatres.'

'In which case, why do you live here? You're a young woman, unmarried. Surely the bright lights have beckoned?'

Sophie afforded him a long, even stare.

'That is my business. Thanks for showing me around

your house and thanks for the tea. I'll be on my way now.'

Before he could respond she turned her back on him and headed out of the door, out of the house, back to the safety of her bicycle which was lying where she had left it.

As she cycled back to her cottage, she tried hard to capture her wayward thoughts and lock them into a compartment in her head. She thought about Christmas, lurking around the corner, about whether she should take advantage of Kat's offer for Jade and her to come to her parents' for lunch, about whether she should do more days at the library now that Jade was at school full time.

But Gregory Wallace kept getting in the way. Admit it, she thought irritably to herself, the man has got under your skin and you resent it because it's something that hasn't happened since Alan. Even with Alan it had been different. Gregory Wallace, she decided, got on her nerves as well as under her skin. Her own in-built suspicion of men, born of bitter experience, managed to deflect some of the forcefulness of his personality, but she was uncomfortably aware of it lying there, waiting to spring out at her.

She spent the next week keeping her head well down and her thoughts on other matters. She had started to accumulate presents for Jade and some of her friends. Jade's she concealed in the attic, and every time she went there to deposit another small something she was startled at quite how much she had managed to collect over a period of weeks. Thank goodness Christmas Day is only a matter of a few weeks away, she thought. Much longer and she would be able to open a small toy shop with the amount of stuff she had bought over time.

She had realised a long time ago that she overcompensated for Jade's lack of a father, but somehow she never managed to deal with the knowledge by cutting back on presents. Christmas was always a time of excess.

She was on her way out of the house two days later when she picked up the mail and opened the one letter to find an invitation inside.

You'd think they would have given up on me by now, Sophie thought, tucking the invitation into her skirt pocket and cycling to the library. It was so cold that she had been forced to wear a jacket over her jumpers. She wished that she had driven her car, which was probably in the process of seizing up due to lack of use.

By the time she got to the library the invitation in her skirt pocket had been completely forgotten, and it remained forgotten until later that evening when Kat came around to dinner and asked in passing whether she had been invited.

'Oh, yes,' Sophie said, tucking into a concoction of rice, vegetables and seafood, which tasted good but had the unfortunate look of something slung together randomly by a child.

'And…?' Kat looked at her expectantly. 'You *are* going to come, aren't you?'

'No.'

Kat rested her head in the palms of her hands and groaned theatrically. 'Have you ever considered that a social life might be quite a good thing for you to have?'

'I *had* a social life, Kat. In London. I found that it disagreed with my system.' Alan had loved nothing better than socialising. He had adored it, and he had been in great demand. Sophie had found herself catapulted out of her natural reticence into a whirl of activity which she had initially found invigorating, then boring and finally horrendously intrusive.

She had hated the false gaiety of everyone she met,

the constant surreptitious competition with the other women, the lack of personal time it afforded her with her husband. It had been a subject of incessant, corrosive argument. Now the thought of dipping her toes into that again filled her with dread.

'Besides,' she said defensively, when her friend continued to stare at her in silence, 'I *have* a social life. Of sorts.'

'You occasionally see a mum from Jade's school for lunch.'

'Sometimes for supper,' Sophie protested, knowing that she was on weak ground because to escalate her social life into anything resembling what a woman of her age should be doing would have necessitated more than simply an exaggeration of the truth.

'Oh, well, I'm surprised you can contain your excitement at it all.'

'That's not fair.'

'You never go to London. When was the last time you met your group of friends from there?'

'A few months ago,' Sophie admitted, stabbing the remainder of her rice with her fork.

'You used to invite them down for weekends now and again. Well, that certainly went out the window.'

'It's hard, doing stuff like that. I'm a mother. What am I supposed to do with Jade?'

'Get someone to babysit?'

'Who? Oh, all right. I know there are people willing to babysit, but—'

'But nothing. Are you busy on the night of the thirtieth of November?'

'I don't believe I am,' Sophie said.

'Then I'll expect you to come. I mean, have a heart, Soph. Who am *I* supposed to chat to for an entire evening at Annabel Simpson's house? You *know* the place will be heaving with all her smart London set and her parents' smart country set. I'll be like a fish out of water.'

'Oh, please!' Sophie said, laughing. 'You are *never* like a fish out of water. You can talk to anyone about anything, even if you know absolutely nothing about the subject in question. Why do you think you're so good at selling houses? You can persuade someone with five homes that they're in dire need of another.'

'So, you're coming, then?'

'What exactly is it in aid of?' Sophie asked, as they rose to clear the table, deciding as she eyed the counter buckling under the weight of unwashed dishes that she would do the lot in the morning.

'Usual pre-Christmas bash,' Kat said airily. 'An opportunity for Annabel and her friends to bedeck themselves in splendid designer clothes and show the rest of us country bumpkins just how drab we all are.'

'Oh, well, that really sounds like the sort of fun social occasion I should be cutting my teeth on.'

'The one last year wasn't too bad,' Kat conceded, making them both a cup of coffee then searching through the cupboard until she located a bar of chocolate. 'There was limitless champagne. I drank enough to see me through the next twelve months.' She bit into her chocolate and looked at her friend thoughtfully. 'Also, I think it's a sort of party to welcome the new boy in town.'

'New boy?'

'The divine Gregory Wallace. You remember him. He was the one who showed you around his house.'

Sophie blushed and wished that Kat would stop staring at her in a suggestive, raised-eyebrows, there's-a-story-here kind of way.

'Which is one reason for me to avoid any party at all costs.'

'Oh, yes? Mind explaining to me?'

Actually, Sophie found that she *did* mind as she couldn't quite explain it to herself. 'I just don't like him,' she said nonchalantly. 'He rubs me up the wrong way. He's too much like Alan.'

'He's nothing like Alan. OK, I'll admit that they have the money thing in common, but that's where the similarity ends. Alan, if you don't mind me speaking ill of your ex, was in love with himself. He thought that he was the sun and everyone else just revolved around him. He also had no time for anyone who didn't pander to his ego, make him look good or could do something for him.'

'And Gregory Wallace is different?' Sophie asked, bitterly aware that the criticism, uncannily accurate, still managed to reflect badly on her.

'You could come and find out. Besides…' Katherine afforded her friend a long, speculative look '…he might just get the wrong impression, you know.'

'Meaning?'

'Well, you know the saying that the lady doth protest too much. He might just think that he has the opposite effect on you if you're anything but indifferent.'

Which, Sophie thought later as she got ready for bed, had been below the belt. How could she argue when Kat might have a point? The last thing she needed to complicate her life was to have Gregory Wallace thinking that he had any effect on her, and he was too good-looking to think otherwise.

Which was why, on the evening of the thirtieth of November, she found herself in her bedroom, staring disconsolately at the few dresses in her possession which she had kept from Alan's days. Most she had got rid of soon after they'd parted company when she'd still been fired with bitterness and rage. Then motherhood had taken over and what remained she had simply stuck in a box in the attic, meaning to send them to a similar fate, only to forget them over the course of the years.

Jade was lying on her bed, fetchingly dressed in a long, cream antique nightie which Sophie had rescued from one of her charity sales months previously, and eyeing each creation her mother tried on with a jaundiced eye.

She pointed to a black affair with a plunging neckline, which was small enough to fit into a powder compact, and Sophie shook her head and mouthed, 'Too tiny.' She made a face and laughed with her daughter.

'What about this one?' she said slowly and clearly, holding up a long, green dress which she remembered as being one of the least provocative ones she had been coerced into buying years ago.

'Yuck. Dull,' Jade wrote on a piece of paper. 'Put on the green one,' she wrote, signing the message, 'I love you, Mummy.' This was followed by a series of kisses and hearts, at which point she appeared to get carried away with the symbols and began to draw lots of smiley hearts floating across the A4 paper.

If Jade thinks it's dull, Sophie decided, that's good enough to me. At least, she thought, it doesn't smell of hibernation in a box. She had had the lot dry-cleaned. Annabel and the rest of her cronies thought she was weird as it was, without adding an odour problem to the list.

She slipped on the dress, without looking at herself in the full-length mirror, and sat at the dressing-table, wondering what to do with her hair. Jade sidled up to her and Sophie recognised that glint in her eye. It was called Operation Hairdresser, one of her least favourite games, but she obediently sat still while her daughter combed her hair with a wide-toothed comb and tried not to grimace too much when tiny fingers intervened to get rid of knots. She should have had the lot chopped off a long time ago, but somehow she had never been able to bring herself to do it.

After fifteen minutes she gave her daughter the thumbs-up sign, even though there was virtually no difference between how her hair looked now and how it had looked previously—still a mass of unruly, undisciplined curls.

Then she applied make-up, something she wore so rarely that she was amazed that her small collection had not gone past its sell-by date.

She brushed on a little powder, dusted with blusher, reluctantly applied mascara and then lipstick. When she sat back and inspected herself she had to admit that she looked good, even though she felt like the Mrs Sophie Breakwell of a few years ago, hanging on the arm of the man who had been the catch of his social circle—someone whose looks had been prized far more highly than her intelligence had been.

The babysitter and Katherine arrived on the doorstep at precisely the same time.

'Wow,' Katherine said in an awe-struck voice, and Sophie sighed in an elaborate way.

'Blame Jade,' she said, letting them in and fetching her ridiculously small clutch bag from the sofa. 'She chose the dress and did the hair. And...' Sophie turned to Ann Warner, who lived a few houses down, '...she shows no signs of being sleepy.' Jade, standing next to her, grinned obligingly even though she hadn't heard the remark.

She knelt, kissed her daughter, informed her that she had better be on best behaviour what with you-know-who arriving down certain chimneys in the not too distant future and then she straightened.

'I'll be back by eleven-thirty,' she said.

'Take your time. I shall enjoy myself with Jade.'

'Yes,' Katherine said, as they walked towards the car, wrapping their coats tightly around them because the cold was numbing, 'you *will* take your time and you *will* enjoy yourself because you will be the *knock-out* of the entire party.'

'And that's an order, is it?' Sophie laughed as she slipped into the passenger seat.

'Absolutely.'

'In which case, I may just as well tell you that I hate taking orders.'

CHAPTER THREE

SOPHIE saw the long line of cars and knew that she wasn't going to enjoy herself.

'I really don't want to be here, Kat,' she said, nurturing the flimsy hope that her friend might suddenly become sympathetic and offer to drive her back home. She felt awkward and uncomfortable in her dress, her shoes were already beginning to make themselves felt and, whatever Kat had said about her appearance, she couldn't help feeling like a clown with all this make-up on.

'Don't be silly,' Kat said briskly, stretching into the back seat of her car and locating her bag. 'I've told you a million times you can't bury yourself in your cottage and pretend that the rest of the world doesn't exist.'

She was right, of course. Sophie knew that, but it didn't help. She could see a group of people entering the stately house, their figures silhouetted against the outside lights—black coats, lots of jewellery, upswept hair. Lots of kisses as they entered, laughing and talking among themselves. More were bringing up the rear, similarly clad, and, from the looks of it, in similar high humour. There was the distant sound of music, a live band, drifting out on the cold air. The trees were all bedecked with hundreds of white lights.

It was all very festive, but Sophie didn't feel festive. She wished that she was back in her own home, curled up on the sofa with Jade half-asleep next to her, reading a book, listening to her daughter and vaguely watching television all at the same time.

'Well?' Kat asked, with her hand on the doorknob. 'Ready?'

'I suppose so,' Sophie said glumly, getting out of the car and dragging her feet as they approached the house.

Annabel's mother was waiting by the door, a short, plump woman who was incongruously and expensively attired in a long, sequinned, vivid blue evening dress. She hugged Katherine, whom she had known since the year dot, and then turned to Sophie with a smile.

'I'm so glad you could come, Sophie,' she said warmly. 'We don't see enough of you.'

Actually, Sophie saw Sheila Simpson quite a bit in and around the village and frequently at the charity events that Sophie organised. Not quite the same, though, she admitted to herself.

'Thank you, Mrs Simpson,' Sophie said, bending so that the older woman could brush her cheek with a kiss. 'How is your husband?'

'Recovering nicely, my dear.' She ushered them in and chatted about Charles, who had recently had a heart attack. 'Of course, he simply loathes taking it easy.'

The older woman's eyes flitted across the massive hall and the moving mass of people, going from one room to another with drinks in their hands. Sophie recognised some of the younger faces as belonging to Annabel's London set. She occasionally saw them around in the village and knew some from years back when Annabel used to bring them to Ashdown during the school holidays when she was back from boarding school.

'Darlings, I must leave you.' She patted Sophie's hand in the manner of someone being kind to an invalid. 'You know your way around, both of you, don't you?'

'Sure, Mrs Simpson,' Kat said, her eyes gleaming. 'We'll just get stuck in.'

'Annabel's somewhere around...' Mrs Simpson's

arms waved about in a vague gesture, but her attention was already on another group of people who were entering.

Kat pulled Sophie away out of the hall. A cloakroom was in operation in one of the downstairs bathrooms, an ornate Victorian affair which was large enough to accommodate three temporary coat rails.

'OK, let's see who's here.'

Sophie nodded. Now that she was here it was ridiculous to droop, and as soon as she saw someone with a tray of champagne she helped herself to a glass and drank it very quickly, which relaxed her slightly— enough so that she could circulate with Kat with at least some semblance of brightness. By the time they stumbled upon Annabel, Caroline and half a dozen of their smart friends she was feeling merry enough to indulge in light-hearted conversation, without her nerves getting too much in her way.

She towered over the other women in the group, as she'd known she would in her heels, but after three glasses of champagne she didn't feel gauche about it. One of the men, a tall, blond man with spectacles and hair that didn't appear to have much of an acquaintance with a comb, was, she acknowledged with a surprising flush of pleasure, more than a little impressed with whatever she was saying.

'Why on earth hasn't Annabel produced you before?' he was asking her, drinking his champagne but with his eyes glued to her face.

'Because, John, darling...' Annabel broke off from what she was saying to Kat and the rest of her entourage '...Sophie hides herself away like a little mole.'

'What an adorable trait,' John said in his cultured voice. 'I've always been rather fond of moles.' That somehow led to a raucous conversation about men and their predilection for ridiculous hobbies, and after a while Kat and Sophie drifted off. They bumped into several other familiar faces, all of whom seemed to be having a roaringly good time.

Supper was served very late. There was a massive table laid with a buffet, the pinnacle of which were six poached salmon, exquisitely adorned with cherry tomatoes and mange-tout.

By this time many people were somewhat under the influence of drink. Conversations were being conducted in voices that were over-hearty and punctuated with very loud bursts of laughter. Kat had managed to disappear in the direction of the music and, after helping herself to a plate of food, Sophie made her way in that general direction.

She was standing at the back of the room, idly watching the frolics on the dance floor and awkwardly trying to manoeuvre food to her mouth with a drink clasped in one hand, when a familiar voice said from next to her, 'I wasn't sure you'd come.'

Sophie felt a shiver of excited apprehension race through her like a sudden electric shock, and she turned to look at Gregory. Thank goodness she had stopped drinking after her third glass of champagne.

'Oh, it's you.'

He was dressed like all the other men in the room in black suit, bow tie and white shirt, but somehow he managed to make a statement in his. He was holding a glass of champagne in his hand and looking at her very carefully and minutely, half smiling.

'Please,' he said with a low laugh, 'do try and keep the delight out of your voice at seeing me.'

Sophie didn't join him in his amusement. She had flirted lightly with some of the men she had run into in the course of the evening but her instincts warned her against flirting with this man, and her instincts were fortunately in good working order at the moment. She refocused her attention on her food.

'I didn't notice you here,' she said, when she had finished eating and had given her plate to one of the circulating waitresses. She drank a very small mouthful of champagne and kept her eyes averted from him.

'And were you overwhelmed with disappointment?'

'Surprisingly, no.'

He laughed, amused by her response.

'Shall we go somewhere less noisy?' he asked, inclining his head towards her so that she could hear him over the din of the music.

Frankly, Sophie couldn't think of anything she would rather not do, and she shot him a glance that said, What do you think?

'In that case,' he said, 'I insist we dance.' He reached out his hand for hers and she gave it a withering glance. Would the man never take the hint?

'I hate dancing.'

'Well, the choice is simple—somewhere quiet where we can talk, without getting laryngitis in the process, or else we dance.'

'*Choice?* What makes you think that I'm about to make a choice between those two options?'

'Because if you don't I shall stamp my feet and scream and throw a tantrum and you'll be terribly embarrassed.'

Their eyes met and she felt a terrible urge to giggle at what he had said.

'Why are you so persistent?'

'It's my gene pool.'

'There must be thousands of women here who would want to talk to you.'

'Thousands might be a slight exaggeration.'

'Well, all right, then. One or two perhaps.'

'Thank you. You're so good for my ego.' He smiled at her with such devastating charm that she felt the colour creep into her face. Men who made passes at her were one thing. John had followed her around for most of the evening, like a puppy, and she could cope with that. Men, however, whose brand of flirting, if that was what it was, awakened a response in her, however slight, were quite a different matter. Gregory, despite the fact that she adamantly told herself that he got on her nerves, fell, infuriatingly, into the latter category.

'Well?' he said, refusing to let the matter drop, 'what is it to be? Dance, quiet spot or I kick and scream?'

'There *are* no quiet spots here,' Sophie told him, and he moved closer.

'It's a vast house. I'm sure we can locate one or two.'

Automatically, Sophie stepped back and looked at him. 'I hate to be rude,' she said, 'but you're infringing my personal space.' She decided that the champagne must have gone to her head more than she had thought because she didn't sound rude at all. She sounded vaguely flirtatious so she frowned to dispel any such impression.

'Oh, dear,' Gregory drawled. 'I must remember to carry a tape measure with me at all times so that I can make sure that the mistake never happens again.'

He took her by her elbow and, because she didn't want to create a scene, Sophie allowed herself to be led out of the noisy room, through the hall, away from the jostling masses and towards one of the sitting rooms, which was far enough away from all the action to be sparsely peopled with a few of the older generation, one of whom was dozing in a chair with a drink in his hand.

'There,' Gregory said with satisfaction. 'Didn't I tell you that we could locate somewhere a little less rowdy?'

Sophie was beginning to wish that she had opted for the dance routine. Here, in this fairly quiet room, she felt trapped in a setting that was far too intimate for her liking. There was nothing to distract her from the man by her side, aside from what remained of her drink—which she swallowed in two gulps, despite her determination to remain totally sober for the rest of the night.

'Are you having a good time?' he asked curiously, taking her empty glass from her and depositing it on the nearby mantelpiece.

Sophie shrugged. 'It's pretty much as I expected,' she said. She paused, and then continued politely, 'What about you? Are you enjoying yourself?'

'They seem an amiable enough crowd of people.'

'You mean because they're all falling over backwards to make a good impression on you?'

'There you go again.' He shook his head impatiently. 'Can you stop digging at me for a few minutes or is that asking for the impossible?'

She remembered what Kat had said about the lady protesting too much and she gave him a bland, indifferent look.

'Mrs Simpson is very sweet,' she said noncommittally, 'and she's renowned in the village for her annual Christmas party.'

'So I gather.' He took a sip from his glass and looked around him. 'I also gather that you're renowned for not coming.'

'You gather *what*? Have you been discussing me with other people?' She felt a curious mixture of astonishment, alarm and pleasure at this. 'You have no right!' she said angrily.

'Why not?' he asked bluntly. He had finished his visual tour of the room and was looking at her.

'Because…' she spluttered, 'because I'm none of your business.'

'You shouldn't live in a village the size of this one if you value your privacy so much,' he told her, with no attempt at an apology or to humour her, by changing the course of the conversation. 'Everyone is everyone else's business in a place like this. You yourself told me that.'

'I resent your nosing into my private affairs.'

'Don't flatter yourself, Sophie.' He gave her a grimly impatient look, and she wondered why he had bothered to single her out if she irritated him so much—as she obviously did, judging from his expression. 'I wasn't *nosing* into your private affairs, as you put it. I happened to bump into Sheila Simpson when I was last here and somehow the subject was mentioned.'

Since there was the slight possibility that he was telling the truth, and since there seemed no point in pursuing a conversation that wasn't going to get anywhere apart from under her skin, she abandoned it completely.

'And how is your house coming along?' she asked him instead. Against her better judgement, she allowed him to refill her glass from one of the bottles on the table. White wine this time, slightly warm but excellent nevertheless. And invigorating for her state of mind, which was beginning to fray slightly at the edges.

'Nicely,' he said. He nodded to two empty chairs by the mantelpiece. 'Care to sit down?' They strolled over to the chairs and sat down. Sophie automatically glanced at her watch. So much for being home by eleven-thirty. It was already a quarter to twelve, and heaven only knew where Kat was.

'In a rush?' he asked, and she sensed rather than saw that he was vaguely irritated by her gesture.

'As a matter of fact I am,' she said. 'I shall have to hunt Kat down in a short while, I'm afraid.'

'I'll give you a lift back to your house.'

'No, thank you.'

'Why not?'

'Because I wouldn't want to drag you away from the party.'

'Will your friend be in a fit state to drive?'

That hadn't occurred to Sophie, but now that she gave the matter some thought, she realised that it was more than possible that they would end up having to take a taxi home. That would mean they would have to book one and the chances of getting one tonight, when they would all be fully booked to ferry guests to the hotel in the village or else back to their homes, didn't look promising.

'I'd better go,' she said abruptly, and stood up, too intent on locating her friend to pay much attention to the fact that Gregory was following her.

By the time she found Kat she realised that any hope of being driven back to her house by her friend was out of the question. She was standing under a sprig of mistletoe. Her cheeks were flushed, and she was on the verge of depositing a kiss on a man whom Sophie had never seen in her life before.

'You said you would stop drinking after two glasses,' Sophie hissed, grabbing Kat by the arm and depriving her friend's companion of his kiss.

'So did you, if I recall.' Kat grinned lopsidedly at her and giggled.

'We'll have to get a cab.' Sophie groaned at the thought of the impossibility of that.

'I told you,' Gregory said from behind her, 'I'll drive the pair of you back to your homes.'

'I'll ferry this one,' the man holding the sprig of mistletoe said. 'I have a driver.'

'Good!' Gregory said, and Sophie looked at all three

faces with dismay. Why was Kat wearing that stupid grin on her face and peering at her in a knowing manner? Couldn't she *see* that Sophie didn't want to be cooped up in a car with Gregory Wallace? Especially when she was tipsy but not tipsy enough to be oblivious to the experience?

'Shall we go?' he said into Sophie's left ear, and she gave an irritated click with her tongue.

'See ya!' Kat winked at her and she looked at her friend coldly, which didn't go any distance to dampening her high spirits.

With her head still fuddled with unease, Sophie found herself going through the rounds of farewells and then the coats and the freezing blast of night air on her face, which would have been enough to have sobered her up if she'd been feeling any lingering effects of alcohol.

'I hope *you're* in a fit state to drive this car,' she said, as soon as Gregory was sitting next to her and starting the engine. 'These country roads can be treacherous in winter, you know. Not like driving in London.'

'Don't be such a damned shrew,' he said, carefully manoeuvring through the courtyard, which was missing a few cars but not very many.

Sophie glanced at him sideways. 'I just don't want to end up in a ditch somewhere. I have a child to look after.'

If he had mentioned her to Mrs Simpson, even in passing, he would almost certainly know of Jade's existence so she wasn't too surprised when he nodded slightly and said, 'Tell me about her.'

'You never got around to telling me about your house,' Sophie said, cutting off any such conversation before it even had a chance to get going. Even though everyone knew about Jade—even though it was no secret—she still didn't want to talk about her daughter to

Gregory Wallace. She knew what she was afraid of. She was afraid of confiding in him. Alan had seen to that. He had taken her trust and had trampled it underfoot, and the thought of opening up to anyone, especially someone like Gregory Wallace, scared her.

'Why don't you want to talk to me about her?'

'You need to take the next left.'

'How old is she?'

'Nearly six.' That one concession was enough to make her nervous of what else might lie in store.

'I know she's deaf.' He spoke softly, in a musing tone. 'That must have been very hard for you.'

'You *told* me that you hadn't been nosing into my life.' Sophie rounded on him accusingly.

'It's not a secret. Why are you so uptight about talking about anything to do with yourself?'

'Because none of it is your business. You don't even live here!'

'And would it make much difference if I did?' He turned left and she briefly gave him the remainder of the directions to her house.

Sophie didn't answer him. Instead, she stared out of the window and watched the passing trees that lined the road, in summer heavy with blossom but now stripped bare.

He sighed, and said, as though the last ten minutes of awkward conversation had never happened. 'Most of the rooms are completely done now. Enough for me to move in, anyway, which—you'll be disappointed to hear—I intend to do. I like it here.'

'Don't be ridiculous,' she snapped, turning to face him. 'Of course you don't.'

They had reached her house now, and he pulled up, but left the engine running. It was a large, expensive car and the noise was like the low, silky purr of a tiger.

'I apologise,' she said in a stilted voice. 'That was uncalled-for.'

'It most certainly was,' he said coolly. 'Mind telling me why you said it?'

Because, she thought, Alan had hated this place and, despite what Kat says, you remind me of him. Less than at first, admittedly, but still enough for certain responses to come out without forethought. How could she explain that? Her past, she knew, was something into which he would have no insight, however much he might have heard about her.

No one knew the full story of her divorce. She had told Kat some of it, but not nearly all, and as far as everyone else was concerned she had simply returned to Ashdown, another victim of a marriage that hadn't worked out. When asked, she shrugged and said that Alan's hours had come between them, and because so many marriages floundered for just that reason no one had pressed her further.

'I don't know why I said it,' Sophie said, facing him and very much aware of how close he was to her. 'I must learn to think before I speak,' she continued, with an attempt at a smile, a smile which he didn't return.

It was too dark to see his expression clearly, but she suspected, uncomfortably, that he was analysing her, try- ing to get inside her mind and work out what made her tick—trying to get to bits of her which were routinely out of bounds for the rest of the human race. She didn't understand why, though she reasoned that that was sim- ply his nature—to persist whenever he found a problem, to persist until the problem was solved. If she had been lively and open then the chances were that he would never have taken more than a passing interest in her.

He turned off the engine and said, 'I'll walk you to

your door, and don't even waste your breath by telling me that there's no need.'

That pretty much forestalled what she had been about to say so she let him walk her to the front door. What could she say when he stepped inside and waited while Ann gathered up her things and related what had gone on that evening, all the while shooting interested looks in his direction?

'There goes your reputation,' he said, ignoring the fact that Sophie had purposely left the front door open for him to leave.

'It's fine for you to go now,' Sophie said. She hadn't removed her coat, but the cold air was wafting in through the door, filling the house. 'It's cold, standing here with the door open.'

'In that case, why don't you shut it?'

'What,' she asked, closing the door furiously and following him into the kitchen, where he seemed to be in the process of making himself at home, 'do you think you're doing?'

'I need a cup of black coffee to wake me up before I drive back.'

'Your house,' she reminded him, 'is under two miles away.' She stood in the doorway of the kitchen with her arms folded. 'I really don't think it's likely that you're going to keel over at the wheel from exhaustion before you get there.'

'I'm driving back to London,' he said, rubbing his eyes with his thumbs.

Sophie hesitated and he didn't look at her.

'Well, all right. One cup of black coffee and then you go because I happen to be very tired and I shall have an early start tomorrow morning.'

'Why? Tomorrow's Sunday.'

'Try telling that to a five-year-old.' She filled the kettle and made them both a cup of coffee, then she sat at the kitchen table opposite him and looked at him over the rim of her cup.

'Where is your ex-husband?' he asked conversationally, and Sophie glared at him.

'Why aren't you married?' she returned swiftly, reckoning that if he could ask awkward questions that didn't concern him then she could do likewise.

'I came close once,' he said, smiling slightly as though he had seen through her ploy, 'but I discovered our incompatibility before I took the plunge.'

'And what was that?' Sophie asked, curious in spite of herself.

'She was more interested in her career than she was in me, and she didn't want children.'

'You want children?'

'Why do you sound so shocked at that? Most men do. Something to do with immortality, so they say.'

'Alan...'

'Didn't want any?'

'Lives in New York,' she said, confused by the admission she had been very close to making. He hadn't wanted children. He disliked them. The pregnancy had been a mistake and he had never forgiven her for it, although that, she knew in retrospect, had not been the reason for the collapse of their marriage, merely the final symptom of something which had been terminally ill anyway. 'He went there as soon as the divorce came through.'

'So your daughter has never met him?'

Sophie drained her cup and stood up. 'No,' she said flatly.

He followed her to the front door and slowly slipped on his coat. 'And what exciting plans have you got for Christmas?' he asked. She breathed a sigh of relief that he wasn't going to continue to pry into her life, although what unsettled her most wasn't his relentless curiosity but her absurd temptation to satiate it. It was ridiculous when she thought how long she had kept herself to herself, never letting go, ridiculous when she thought how inappropriate a confidant Gregory Wallace would be.

'This and that,' Sophie said vaguely. 'I've planned a few things for Jade.' She paused and added politely, 'And yourself?'

'Oh, this and that,' he said, echoing her vagueness. He was standing with his back to the door and looking down at her. 'Getting ready to move into the house.'

'Oh, you've set a date for that, have you?' She wondered what that would entail. Would she see more of him? The thought of that filled her with apprehension, but mingled with that was a thread of anticipation as well, which she tried to disregard.

'Early in the new year.' He paused and looked at her with his hands in his coat pockets. 'I shall have a small housewarming party. Will you come?'

'I shouldn't think so,' Sophie answered bluntly.

'Why not?'

'I dislike parties. But thank you for the invitation.'

'You don't believe in skirting around the truth, do you?' he asked coolly.

'Why should I? People can end up in unfortunate situations when they try and skirt around the truth.' The truth was that she had always hated parties. She was someone who felt far more comfortable in the company of a few people rather than many. If she'd established that from the start when she'd met Alan, instead of meekly going along with his suggestions, their affair might well have fizzled out. He wouldn't have become bored and intolerant of her, and she wouldn't have ended up so utterly disenchanted with men.

'Fine.' He opened the door and stepped outside. 'I'll see you around.'

'Doubtless,' she replied, watching him for a few seconds as he strode down the path towards his car. She quietly shut the door and continued to look at it for a much longer time.

She had made her point. She had informed him in no uncertain terms that she was a recluse, more or less, who enjoyed her reclusivity. So why was there such a dry, unsatisfied taste in her mouth? Why did she feel that the conversation had ended on a sour note? More to the point, why did she care one way or the other? But she found that she did.

She had been more than simply abrupt, she thought. She had been unnaturally rude, and that wasn't like her. She valued her privacy, but she wasn't the completely anti-social beast which she had somehow managed to make herself out to be. She could smile, she could laugh, she could enjoy other people's company, even though she might not envy their lifestyles. So how, exactly, had she succeeded in making such an extraordinarily bad impression of herself in the eyes of Gregory Wallace?

As Christmas drew closer, and the tree was put in place, with all the attendant gifts scattered around it, Sophie found herself half wishing that she would run into Gregory somewhere—*anywhere*. At the back of her mind was some blurry intention to be nice, to prove to him that she could be. She took Jade to the local pantomime, which she followed, understanding what was going on through the frolics on stage.

By Christmas Eve Sophie was ever so slightly depressed, even though she told herself that being nice to Gregory Wallace was the last thing she should be thinking of doing. Her head had told her to steer a wide berth from him, and her head couldn't possibly be wrong because it was what prevented people from making rash decisions instead of sensible ones.

Still, on Christmas Day, after all the excited unwrapping of presents had been done and she was standing in Kat's parents' kitchen, helping Kat to do the dishes, while everyone else, all fifteen of them—assorted family and friends—were allowing their self-indulgent lunchtime excesses to digest, she couldn't help asking whether he was around.

She wasn't looking at Kat when she asked this. She was concentrating heavily on drying a plate.

'Why? I thought you couldn't stand the man,' Kat said, immediately using the question as an excuse to stop washing. She carefully removed her rubber gloves and folded her arms.

'Just curious,' Sophie said, wishing that she hadn't brought up the subject. After the Simpsons' party she had managed to stave off all her friend's questions with indifferent shrugs, and she had made sure that his name wasn't mentioned so that the matter of what had gone on during that drive back had been finally dropped.

'Oh, yes.' Kat nodded speculatively.

'And there's no need to look at me like that. I was just making polite conversation, for goodness' sake! I'm just as happy to talk about Jade's Christmas presents or…or…that meal we had out last week with Claire and Angie or…or…*whatever*!'

'He moves in in ten days' time. He's been in London most of the time, but he'll be around pretty soon. In fact, I wasn't going to mention it but he dropped by my office a few days ago with an invitation to a party he's having.'

Sophie felt as though she had been punched in her stomach.

'Oh. Really.' She had finally finished with the plate

and she took another from the draining-board, this time lavishing even more attention on it so that Kat couldn't see her face and read the expression in her eyes.

Sophie had never felt so confused in her life before. She hadn't been invited, and she knew why. She had told Gregory point blank that she wasn't interested in going to any house-warming party so why did she feel so *upset* because he had taken her at her word?

'He didn't…ask you…?' Now Kat looked as upset as her friend felt, and Sophie smiled nonchalantly.

'He mentioned that he would be having a do of sorts and I told him that I wasn't interested.'

'But you are.'

'I'm not,' Sophie said fiercely. 'I really am not,' she said in a more normal tone. 'You'll have to tell me all about it afterwards. Who wore what. You know.'

'Come with me, Soph. He'd love to see you. I'm sure he…you know…'

'What?' This time she deposited the plate on the counter and looked her friend fully in the face.

'I think you fascinate him.'

Sophie laughed. 'And I think you have an imagination that's way too fertile for its own good.'

If I fascinated him that much, she thought later in bed, he would have asked me, and it's a relief that I don't. It's a relief because I don't need complications in my life.

She turned onto her side and looked at Jade who was sleeping on the bed next to her, along with an assortment of Christmas presents, none of which were suitable for a sound night's sleep.

I have my daughter, she told herself. She's all I shall ever need.

CHAPTER FOUR

THE telephone had to ring eight times before Sophie got there to answer it. She had been in the middle of cleaning the house, which looked like a tip. A seemingly unreasonable number of Barbie dolls and their various thousands of accessories appeared to be staging a complete take-over of all available free space, despite Sophie's attempts to get Jade to pack them all away after use.

The ironing had grown to towering heights in the basket in the laundry room. There was washing to be done. All that was on top of small incidentals, like having to prepare something for them both to eat later that evening. So when she picked up the receiver she was not in the best of moods.

'Yes?' she snapped.

'Caught you at a bad moment, have I?'

Sophie heard the dark, charming voice down the line, and her heartbeat accelerated furiously in response.

'I'm in the middle of doing the housework,' she said, sitting on the arm of the sofa and idly gazing at Jade who was in the process of extricating her dolls and bundling them on the coffee-table in an array of artificial poses. 'What do you want?' she asked, twisting the spiral cord of the phone in her fingers.

Why, she wondered, was it so impossible to sound natural with him? Why did every nerve in her body immediately go into overdrive the minute she heard his voice or saw his face? It was irritating, to say the least.

'Yes, I had a very enjoyable if a little hectic Christmas, thank you. How about you?'

She wished he would get to the point. He surely hadn't rung to make a social call. If he had telephoned to invite her to his wretched party then she would know that Kat had mentioned something to him and had given him totally the wrong idea, insinuating that Sophie was disappointed not to be going. If that was the case, she would slam down the receiver and strangle her friend.

'I wish you'd tell me why you called me,' she said. 'I'm very busy and—'

'I've been told that you do catering,' he replied flatly.

'Oh.' She paused. 'And what if I do?'

'Oh, for God's sake. I will not use it as evidence against you in a court of law. Do you or do you not do catering?'

'Yes,' Sophie admitted. She stood up, stretched her limbs and then sank onto the sofa, tucking her feet beneath her.

'Good. I want you to do the catering for the small house-warming party you refused to attend.'

'Why?'

She heard him groan and felt a twinge of guilt at her pigheadedness.

'Because,' he said very slowly, 'the only other place in the village that can help me out is the hotel and they're busy. As are the caterers I normally use in London. Your name cropped up and I phoned on the off chance that you might be able to oblige. Is that a thorough enough explanation for you or would you like it in writing?'

Sophie thought for a few seconds. She enjoyed cooking and did it on a small-time basis. 'What sort of numbers did you have in mind?' she asked cautiously.

'In the region of twenty-four.'

'I'm afraid I only have experience in catering locally. I'm sure I won't be up to the standard you're accustomed to.'

'It might be nice if you let me decide that.'

'When is this for?' she asked, as though she didn't already know, thanks to Kat, and he gave her the date. It was in ten days' time when everyone should have recovered from New Year's Day and any hangovers they might be nursing.

'It doesn't give me a great deal of time,' she prevaricated, half wishing he would remove the decision-making process from her, by telling her that he would look elsewhere.

'Are you going to take this job or not?' he demanded impatiently, and she made her mind up.

'I suppose I could…'

'Good. I shall want you to arrange some help for serving the food and drinks. Is that possible?'

'I'll try my best.'

He muttered something under his breath along the lines of hoping that she never considered a career in selling, which she chose to ignore.

'What do you want?'

'I already told you what I wanted!' he exploded.

'I meant,' Sophie said serenely, ignoring this outburst as well, 'what would you like me to cook for you and your guests? Hot? Cold? Buffet? Sit-down? What?'

'Whatever. I'll leave it to you.'

'That's not good-enough.'

'Oh, all right. Sit-down, then. Hot.'

'Beef, pork, chicken, lamb, venison or other?'

'A selection.'

'Of all?'

'Are you doing this to be difficult?'

'No.'

'Chicken. Lamb. Both. And trimmings. You *can* sort out the trimmings without me going into detail, can't you?'

'What about crockery?'

'No need to arrange that. I have.'

'Fine. I shall come in some time in the morning around eleven.'

'I'll be there.'

'And I work best when left to my own devices,' she added, just in case he got it into his head that hovering might be a good idea.

'I wouldn't have expected anything less,' he answered. He proceeded to tell her how much he would pay, and when she protested that it was far too much he informed her that it was what he paid his caterers in London.

'Who are experienced,' she pointed out.

'Oh, good grief. I'll see you in a few days' time.' Upon which he replaced the receiver. Sophie returned to Jade's antics with her dolls, her head half full of menus and half full of the man who had just called her.

Chicken with olives and mushrooms. Lamb in a redcurrant sauce. An assortment of vegetables, which she hoped would be highly ornamental because of their colours. Two salads. Rolls, freshly made.

Sophie found herself shopping enthusiastically for the ingredients and looking forward to doing the cooking. It had been nearly three months since she had done any catering. The last time had been for a ladies' bridge luncheon party, which had been hosted by Lady Straw, and it had gone beautifully.

This was, she had to admit, a slightly different kettle of fish, especially as Gregory Wallace would be accustomed to the very best, but she tried not to let that daunt her.

On the morning in question she bundled herself and Jade into her car, along with three boxes of ingredients, and drove to Gregory's house.

It was snowing. It wasn't enough to be a problem, and she hoped that it would stay that way. Snow had a tendency to get completely out of hand in these parts. Light flurries could develop into awesome drifts in a matter of a couple of hours and, apart from anything else, it would be a shame if Gregory's dinner party had to be abandoned because of bad weather.

They ran to the door together and rang the bell. It was answered immediately by Gregory, who bustled them into the house.

'Your daughter.' He half closed the door and looked down at the diminutive red-haired child, holding her mother's hand. Jade was likewise staring up at him in frank curiosity.

Sophie hadn't originally wanted to drag her daughter along. It would be boring for her and, aside from that, she felt reluctant to allow Gregory this further insight into her personal life. But common sense had told her she was being silly. Jade wasn't some deep, dark secret.

'Jade,' Sophie told him. She took a deep breath. 'She's deaf.'

'I know.'

'You seem to know a lot about me.'

'Nothing that everyone else in this village doesn't know.' He looked at her. 'Why are you so secretive with me? We're practically neighbours now.'

'Which doesn't entitle you to my biography.'

He didn't answer that. Instead, he stooped and very slowly told Jade to make herself at home. 'Does she understand sign language?' he asked, still stooping but glancing towards Sophie, and she nodded.

'A bit. She's getting better at it. I try and do a little with her every day.'

He stood up. 'Are your things in the car?'

'The boot. I'll just go out—'

'Give me the key.'

She handed it to him and watched from inside, with her coat still on, as he made three trips into the house, depositing bags of groceries in the hall. Then he shut the front door, rubbing his hands together.

'I'll get started,' Sophie said, removing her coat and vaguely wondering where she could hang it. He wasn't staring at her, and she caught the expression on his face from little more than a brief, sideways glance, but it was enough to tell her that he was looking at her and comparing her to how she had looked at the Simpsons' party when she had been dressed to the nines. Whoever had said that what mattered was what lay under the surface? She would bet her last pound coin that any comparisons he was making were unfavourable. He was probably finding it hard to believe that she was the same person.

She wore no make-up, her hair hung in two braids down her back and she was wearing dungarees and an old jumper underneath because cooking was hardly an activity suited to designer clothes—not that she possessed any. And her favourite lace-up ankle boots. Practical shoes for the weather. The sort of outfit that Alan had refused to allow her to wear. Even when it had just been the two of them, he had preferred her to dress expensively, as though at any given moment they might be descended on by an army of People in High Places.

He took her coat, hung it over the banister, and after all the food had been lugged into the kitchen she turned to him with her arms folded.

'I know,' he said dryly. 'You work best when you're

left alone. You made that perfectly clear on the telephone.'

Sophie blushed with embarrassment at this reminder
of her abruptness with him.

'Jade will be fine in the kitchen with me,' she said.
'I've brought her some books and puzzles and crayons.'

'I'll show her around the house,' Gregory said, and
she immediately opened her mouth in protest. 'Before
you say another word, why don't we ask her what she'd
like to do?' He squatted alongside Jade and explained
that he wanted to show her a room full of teddy bears.
Would she like to see it?

Jade nodded vigorously, and looked at her mother.

'You have a room full of *teddy bears*?' Sophie asked
incredulously.

'A legacy from my mother. She collected them.'

Jade's look was going from questioning to imploring
and Sophie gave in. 'All right,' she said, 'but please
don't feel that you have to—'

'Shut up.' He straightened and looked her in the eye.
'Much better,' he said with satisfaction, as Sophie remained where she was with her mouth half-open. He
held out his hand, and Jade slipped hers into it. Then
they vanished out of the kitchen, and with a short sigh
of frustration and disbelief that *anyone* could be so rude
Sophie began to unpack and get things in order.

She had no idea how long they were gone. She was
totally involved in the cooking. His kitchen was large
and well equipped, but the bottle-green Aga gave it a
warm, homely atmosphere. At some point between the
proving of the bread and the preparation of the chicken
Jade flew into the kitchen, gave her a quick kiss and
flew back out with a puzzle under her arm. At a little
after twelve-thirty Gregory strolled in with Jade and told
her to stop.

'Because it's lunch,' he said, 'and we have to eat.'

'I'll make Jade a sandwich, if that's all right, and I'll carry on…'

'I'll take her out for a burger.' He mouthed 'burger' at her, and Jade nodded rapturously.

'Don't be ridiculous,' Sophie snapped.

'Is that your quaint way of saying thanks?'

'It's my quaint way of saying there's no need. You must have *other* things to do!'

'Don't be ungrateful and churlish.'

Which was precisely how she felt, and that only made her madder.

'Please?' Jade mouthed, and Sophie shot Gregory a frustrated look from under her lashes.

'Get back to your cooking,' he said, 'and admit defeat.'

They left her fuming amid the pots and pans, even though she thought that it was nice. Nice for Jade, who was clearly lapping it up. Nice for Gregory, who would end the day with a comfortable feeling of having started the new year on a good deed. Not so nice for her because she felt mean and the villain of the piece.

By the time they returned two hours later—two hours for a burger—the cooking was well under way and the kitchen looked less of a bombsite than it had done forty minutes previously.

She made a fuss of Jade, sat her down at the kitchen table with one of her jigsaw puzzles and then looked across at Gregory, who was peering into pots and under lids and making appreciative sounds.

'I've managed to get three girls from the village to help out this evening. They'll be coming around seven o'clock. I shall leave around six to drop Jade off at the babysitter, then I'll be back to see to things.' She wiped her hands on her apron, checked a couple of pots and then, when he showed no inclination to vacate the kitchen, turned to him and said briskly, 'Is that all right? I'm not sure what the procedure is when your London caterers take over.'

'Jade is a delightful child,' he said, looking at her. 'You did a good job, bringing her up. It must have been hard on your own.'

The unexpectedness of the comment made her flush and for a second she couldn't think of anything to say, although she was aware of a swift stab of pleasure at his compliment.

'Well…' she said uncertainly, taken aback. She gave a nervous little laugh, for once not inclined to slap him down for making a personal remark. She felt hot and pleasantly exhausted.

'Why don't you sit down and relax for a few minutes?' he suggested, moving away from her and pouring himself a glass of water from the tap. Sophie looked at him as he turned away from her to drink the water in one gulp—at the graceful curve of his back, the inherent strength in his arms, an impression of beauty in motion. Then she blinked and wondered whatever she was thinking.

She did something with the sauce simply so that she didn't have to continue to look at him.

'Sit,' he said. 'Relax.'

'You were gone a while,' Sophie said, making herself a cup of tea and hurriedly drinking it in what she hoped looked like a relaxed pose. She could feel every nerve in her body tense from the effort of trying not to react to him.

'We had a short tour of the village after the burger to walk off the fat content.'

'There really was—'

'No need. So you already told me. Why did your husband walk out on you and Jade?'

'What?'

'I take it that your answer to that is that it's none of my business.'

'Damn right!'

'Are you going to join everyone tonight?'

'No,' Sophie said, destabilised by his clever footwork with the conversation. She didn't know whether to be annoyed with him, relieved that he had dropped the possibility of an uncomfortable topic or merely surprised by his audacity at touching on such a personal subject in the first place. 'There'll be too much to do in the kitchen,' she explained, supporting her elbow with one hand while she tried to gulp down her tea as rapidly as possible.

'Bit awkward for you, don't you think? Considering you'll know more or less everyone there?'

'I'm accustomed to that,' Sophie answered with a shrug. 'Now, if you don't mind,' she said, depositing her cup in the sink, folding her arms and tilting her face to look at him. 'I have a few more things to do...' She gesticulated in the general direction of the Aga, and he frowned with the irritation of someone unaccustomed to being given the brush-off. 'Then Jade and I will be out of your hair and I'll return at around seven to get things under way.'

'How are you going to get here?'

'Well, now,' Sophie said, leaning back against the counter and tapping her finger on her chin. 'I wonder... Should I walk? Jog? Roller-skate? Dust down my helicopter and use that...? Oh, I know! I'll use my car!'

'Do you *ever* answer a straight question with a straight reply?'

'It was a stupid question.'

His eyebrows flew up at that and she remembered that he was probably unused to anyone being sarcastic to him. No wonder she got on his nerves.

'It's snowing,' he said. 'You drive a sewing machine with an engine. How reliable is that in snow?'

'It's not snowing that heavily.' She had drawn the curtains in the kitchen because it was already dark even though it had only just gone four-thirty. Now she strolled over and peeped outside where the light flurries had thickened slightly. 'My sewing machine should just be able to manage the drive over,' she said, letting the curtain drop back and glancing down at her daughter who was engrossed with her colouring. She had an annoying habit of trying to lick her felt-tip pens back into life and her mouth was stained blue. Sophie absent-mindedly tilted Jade's face, pointed to her mouth and then waggled one finger in admonishment.

'And what about driving back?' Gregory asked patiently. 'I have a Range Rover. I could come and collect you when you're ready.'

'No, thanks,' Sophie said dismissively.

'Fine.' He shrugged, looked at his watch and informed her that he would be in his study if she needed him. If not, he would see her later. Then he strolled over, said goodbye to Jade and left the kitchen.

That was the last Sophie thought about snow. True, when she got outside forty minutes later it really was thicker than it had been earlier on, but she had become accustomed to fairly ferocious blizzards in this part of the country and what she was looking at was mild in comparison to some she'd experienced.

She drove Jade over to the babysitter, who had thoughtfully prepared Jade's favourite array of pre-packaged food, then she dashed back to her house to change. She had considered staying for the duration in her dungarees and having a very late bath when she returned, but the prospect of a shower was irresistible. Besides, she admitted to herself, she would be in the company of people she knew, even if she *was* going to be behind the scenes, and the thought of appearing, however fleetingly, in clothes most people would expect to find at Oxfam did not appeal.

Not that she intended to dress for the occasion, but her long skirt was a deep green instead of black, her top was fitted instead of baggy and her jumper had a few colours in it, even if it did still conform to her normal style of jumper, which was loose and long. Less bag-lady, she thought, grinning at herself in the mirror, and more bohemian. She tied her hair back to keep it away from her face, then slowly manoeuvred her car down the familiar road back to Gregory's house.

Gregory was nowhere around when she arrived. One of the girls whom she had employed for the evening opened the door to her, and Sophie smiled.

'I wondered whether you would make it,' she said, shrugging out of her coat and taking it to the kitchen with her. 'Are Jane and Sara here yet?'

'Came with me,' Karen said from behind her, 'Jane's mum dropped us off in her car, and I'm afraid we're going to have to leave as soon as the dishes are in the kitchen, Sophie. Jane's mum's nervous about the weather. She said if we leave it too late she might not be able to get out for us. Actually, what I think she meant was if we left it too late she would fall asleep and forget all about us altogether.'

'OK.' She was barely listening. Most of the hard work was finished, but there was still all the fiddly stuff to be done. Fortunately, all three had worked for her before and knew her routine. While she added cream to things and began the process of making sure that everything would reach the table piping hot and artistically arranged, they removed themselves to the dining room and efficiently began to lay the table with the crockery which had been set out for their disposal.

Every so often Sophie consulted her watch, hearing the distant rustle of people arriving. When Gregory strode into the kitchen at a little after eight things were going smoothly.

She turned as she heard him approach and had to stop herself from staring. He was wearing cream trousers, which, in Ashdown in the dead of winter, was daring to the point of madness, and a cream shirt. He looked casual and elegant and, she had to face it, overwhelming.

She couldn't remember Alan ever possessing a pale pair of trousers. He had always managed to look like a city gent even when relaxing. At first she had found that exciting before it began to get on her nerves, just as most things about him had started getting on her nerves ever so slightly.

'Has everyone arrived?' Sophie asked, making a point of keeping her eyes on his face.

As if on cue, Kat arrived in the company of the Simpsons, and after ten minutes of conversation Sophie shooed them out of the kitchen. 'One of the drawbacks of catering for people you know,' she explained to Gregory, who had not similarly seen fit to leave.

'You'll have to make an appearance to keep them all at bay,' he responded.

'I'll see them in passing,' Sophie replied. 'Now, please go and entertain your guests. You're getting in my way and, besides, it's rude not to be out there.' She couldn't concentrate with the man around.

He vanished and she breathed a sigh of relief. From then onwards everything seemed to run on automatic. The food was brought out to twenty-four delighted peo-

ple who insisted on filling her in on the village gossip
which had accumulated over the Christmas period. Sara
played waitress, topping up glasses as they emptied.
Then came dessert, then cheese, followed by coffee. It
was after midnight before the first of the guests apolo-
gised for having to leave.

'Before the snow gets too ridiculous,' he explained,
dragging his wife away from an animated conversation
with one of her neighbours.

After that there was a rapid exodus. Kat pulled her
aside and said, *sotto voce*, 'I take it you're staying on to
do the dishes, oh, great master chef?'

'All part of the job,' Sophie said, grinning.

'Hmm. Interesting.'

'What is?'

'Well, as yet nothing, but who knows…?'

'Go. Away. Kat. Or I'll never cook another meal for
you again.'

'You certainly know how to hit below the belt. Have
I told you that my diet went completely haywire over
Christmas and I've put on seven pounds?'

'No, and you can tell all when I see you on
Wednesday.'

'Likewise, I'm sure,' Kat said, smirking and casting
her eyes in Gregory's direction.

It was only when the house was completely empty
and her three efficient helpers had departed, after profuse
apologies for leaving her with most of the washing-up,
that Sophie began to feel nervous.

Gregory had come into the kitchen to help tidy away,
even though she had virtually begged him not to. 'And,'
he informed her, 'I'm taking you back to your house in
my car. It's a four-wheel drive so it should be able to
manage weather like this.'

Sophie didn't argue. When the last of the guests had

left she had looked out of the front door and had seen that the picturesque flurries of snow had degenerated into an alarmingly heavy fall, which was collecting ominously on the ground.

'In fact,' Gregory said, drying as fast as she could wash, 'why don't you leave this lot and I'll drop you back now?'

'Because I'm paid to do a full job,' she answered stubbornly.

'You're being ridiculous.'

'I'll go now if you cut my money.'

'Ridiculous to the point of insane.'

'In that case, I'll stay and hope that the snow slows up a bit.'

'What about Jade?'

'I'm collecting her in the morning.' The plates were finished. Now came the glasses, of which there seemed to be hundreds.

They worked in silence for a while, with Sophie feeling increasingly aware of him next to her, then she said politely, 'And how did the evening go?'

'Very well, I think. Nice slice of humanity, and I've seen enough of humanity to make the comparison.'

'Am I supposed to ask you to enlarge on that?' She lifted the roller blind by the sink to peer outside. 'This weather is a mess. I wish I lived in the South of France,' she added gloomily. 'It doesn't snow there.'

'Why *did* you choose to settle down here?'

Sophie hesitated, but she didn't feel inclined to argue with him. It was warm and cosy in the kitchen, with the snow streaming down outside and no sounds except for the occasional blustery gust of wind rattling against the windowpanes. It was not a night made for arguments.

'Your curiosity,' she said, pausing for a moment to look up at him, 'is like water, dripping on a stone. Do you think that after a while you're going to wear me down?'

'Yes.'

'Why are you so interested, anyway? Don't you have more important things on your mind?'

'You intrigue me,' he said casually, without looking at her.

'The homing instincts of the salmon intrigue me,' she replied with honeyed sarcasm, 'but that doesn't mean that I'm going to devote all my time to finding out more about it.'

'Well, may you never regret your decision.' He paused and then added idly, 'You lived in London with your husband.'

'The village grapevine, I take it?'

'It certainly gets around, doesn't it?'

'Yes, if you really must know, I lived in London with Alan. He would never have dreamed of moving here.'

'Why not?'

'He didn't think that the country life was compatible with someone in the fast lane.'

'Did you bury yourself away here because you needed to recover from him?'

'You're overstepping the mark, Mr Wallace.' She began to wipe the kitchen counters, then she whipped off her gloves, stuck them into one of the bags she was carrying back with her and turned to him.

When she faced him she had her arms folded and she was standing at the far end of the kitchen—away from him and that insidious persuasiveness that he seemed to possess in such abundance. It was as though the closer she got to him physically the more powerful the temptation became to tell him everything he wanted to know, to drop all her defences. What a joke that would be. She had done that once with a man and the experience had been enough to last her a lifetime.

'I'm pretty much finished here ñow,' she said, side-stepping the possibility of any further probing. 'If it's all right with you, I think we ought to leave now, that is if you haven't changed your mind about dropping me home.'

'Let's go.' He tossed the dishcloth onto the counter, fetched his Barbour from where it was hanging on a hook behind the kitchen door and waited until she was similarly togged up.

The weather hit them like a wave the minute they stepped out of the front door. The snow, which had seemed somehow atmospheric from behind the kitchen window, now appeared menacingly thick. The wind blew it into their faces and they had to run to the car, slamming the doors behind them.

He started the engine and very carefully circled the courtyard, before manoeuvring the car down the drive with painstaking care.

'Amazing,' he said, as he drove slowly down the lane. 'It never snows like this in London.'

'The charm will wear thin after you've spent a couple of winters here,' Sophie said. It had never worn thin on *her*, but she still suspected that Gregory was just playing at the rural lifestyle, enjoying the novelty of swapping his suit and tie for boots and a Barbour.

'Back to your crystal ball, I see,' he said with a certain grimness in his voice.

'If this continues we'll all be snowbound by morning.'

'It *is* morning.' They seemed to be getting nowhere fast. The wind was blowing the snow furiously against the windscreen, and the wipers, even at full speed, weren't doing a great deal for visibility. After five minutes and several yards of painstaking driving, he said, 'This will never do.'

Sophie didn't reply. She was busy, looking out of her window and trying to calculate how long it would take her to walk to collect Jane in the morning. Thank heaven she was only a few doors away.

'Did you hear me?' he grated, scrunching the car to a complete stop. 'We can't make it. You're going to have to spend the night at my place.'

This time she heard all right and her head swung round in horror.

'What?'

'It's no go. There are no main roads between here and your house and I can't see a thing through the windscreen.' He twisted around and began to reverse back up the lane from which they had come.

'*I am not spending the night at your house!*' Sophie shouted in panic.

'You don't have much choice.' He glanced at her, his mouth drawn into a tight line of exasperation. 'Or rather you do. You can walk back to your house, if you want to take the chance on getting back in one piece.' They were back in front of his house now. He killed the engine and looked her fully in the face.

'I have no idea what your problem is, lady, but I, for one, am not risking life and limb to try to get you back to your place, which is utterly unnecessary.'

'You've barely made an effort,' she insisted desperately. 'I have a child to consider.'

'Who is with a babysitter, and was going to be there overnight anyway.' He opened his car door, slammed it behind him and began to stride towards the front door. 'Get inside, Sophie!' he commanded as he unlocked the door, 'and stop being an obstinate fool.'

She got out and eyed him with fury through the snow and darkness.

'All right!' she yelled back at him. 'You win. But,' she added, running up to the door which he was holding open for her, 'you could have made it!'

CHAPTER FIVE

SOPHIE handed her coat to Gregory, stood back and folded her arms.

'Well, now that I'm here, perhaps you could show me where you intend to put me?'

He didn't say anything. He walked at a leisurely pace to the downstairs cloakroom, hung up her coat, as well as his own, then turned to her and said calmly, and with a little amusement, 'You look as though you're about to explode. Surely spending one night under this roof isn't such an ordeal?' He leaned against the doorframe and regarded her coolly.

Sophie stared back at him. Now that it was a *fait accompli*, what was the point in protesting? And he was perfectly right, of course. She was sharing a house for one night with a civilised human being, not being thrown into a cage with a wild animal at the height of feeding time. She smiled stiffly and ran her fingers through her hair.

'I'm afraid I'm not accustomed to spending the night away from home, and I had rather banked on getting back.'

'Would you like a nightcap?' He strolled in her direction and she felt her body tense, even though the polite smile remained on her face.

'No, thank you.'

'It'll help you unwind.'

'I don't need help, unwinding. The minute I fall into bed my eyes close and within five minutes I'm asleep.'

'In which case, you're very lucky.' He headed towards

the sitting room, and because she had no idea where she was supposed to be sleeping she reluctantly followed him, eyeing her watch *en route*. It was after one. She should be feeling exhausted, but she wasn't. She felt keyed up and alert. She supposed that the adrenaline rush which had been coursing through her body all evening would take time to subside.

'Sure you won't join me?' he asked, moving towards an ornamental bar. Closed, it resembled a piece of furniture but when opened it revealed bottles of every description, as well as glasses.

'I suppose I could have a...' she tried to think of something alcoholic which might possibly send her off to sleep in a strange bed with speed '...gin and tonic.' That would be a first. She had always steered clear of shorts, but it was unlikely that there was any wine in the bar and she couldn't think of anything else.

'The food was delicious,' Gregory said, handing her the drink and motioning for her to sit down.

She regarded the sofa, with Gregory perched at one end, with misgiving.

'I don't bite. How many times do I have to tell you that?'

'Thank you, I'm glad you enjoyed it,' she said, ignoring the irony and sitting on the sofa.

'Where did you learn to cook?'

'I did a catering degree,' she said, feeling that familiar caution as she imparted the information.

'Where?'

'The Midlands.'

'And then...?'

'And then I knew how to cook.' She took a very generous sip of her drink and felt it rush to her head, like a hand grenade being detonated. 'How strong is this drink?' she asked, holding it up to the very subdued centre light and squinting at it dubiously.

'Not very.' He drank rather more slowly from his glass and continued to eye her over the rim. 'And then?' he prompted. 'You decided to go to…?'

'London.'

'Why not back here?'

'Why are you asking me so many questions?'

'Social intercourse. You must have heard of it. It usually involves getting to know someone.'

'Oh, really. Thank you for that piece of insight.' She finished the remainder of her drink, enjoying the fiery sensation it produced while disliking the taste. 'Why did *you* decide to go to London?'

'Because I burned with the ambition to corner the biggest market in thc UK,' he said, looking for her reaction to that, and she gave a predictable grimace of distaste. 'I thought you might have something to say about that,' he said, as he swirled his drink in his hand, an annoying glimmer of a grin on his face.

'I didn't say anything.'

'You didn't have to. Your face said it all on your behalf.' He got up to pour himself another, and reached out for her glass. On cue, she told him that she was tired and should be getting to bed. Actually, she didn't feel tired. She felt lazy and comfortable. Outside, she could see the snow, swirling down unabated and blanketing everything in white.

'As a matter of fact,' he said, fetching her glass and refilling it with more of the same, 'I was living in New York until a few years ago, and doing very nicely. Then my father died and my duties brought me back here to take over the running of his company.'

He handed her another drink and because she couldn't be bothered to do what she knew she ought to do, namely stand up and insist that he show her to her room, she sipped from it with a little sigh of reckless resignation.

'New York,' she mused thoughtfully. 'London…Ashdown village. Doesn't quite fit in, does it?'

'The fast lane can get tiring after a while. Occasionally it's nice to wind down somewhere where the pace is a little more sedate.'

'Oh, is that the reasoning?' She gave a short, faintly incredulous laugh and saw his eyes narrow, although his expression remained bland.

Alan used to talk about a country house as well, but such ideas had soon evaporated after he'd visited Ashdown and discovered that country life did not automatically include smart neighbours with fast, sport cars and quaint little shops on the high street, bulging with designer bric-à-brac.

'Why don't you just get it off your chest?' he said with sudden coolness in his voice.

She didn't pretend to misunderstand, and for the first time she felt a deep, desperate urge to tell this man about what life had been like with Alan once the honeymoon had ended. She had no idea if it was because she had drunk two gin and tonics very quickly or because she had kept so much bottled up inside her for such a long time—she just wanted to confide in him.

'You talk about living in the country as though it's some sort of rustic idyll.' she said, standing up and pacing the room restlessly. When she got to the large, double-fronted bay window she paused, staring out into the black, snowy night and half seeing her reflection in the window. There was something snug and reassuring about being inside a warm room when the weather outside was playing its ferocious games.

She turned back and faced him, perching against the window-ledge and folding her arms.

'And you've made such a heroic effort, getting to know everyone, but you'll soon get bored—bored when the skies aren't blue, bored when the birds aren't singing, bored when you want to throw a fancy dinner party and there's no convenient delicatessen nearby, bored when this white snow turns to grey slush and you have to tramp through it and get your expensive trousers dirty on the way to your car, bored when you want to use a flash sports centre and the only thing available is Mrs Farley's aerobics class in the village hall.'

'Because your husband would have?'

'That's right,' Sophie said fiercely. She could feel tears spring to her eyes and she blinked in an effort not to lose control.

Why had this man come here? Why couldn't he have seen fit to choose some other poor, forgotten village for his damned housing estate? Why did he have to buy a house and play the part-time resident? If he had had to build, why couldn't he just have vanished once his mission had been completed? Why, why, why?

'Do you want to talk about it?'

'What's there to talk about?' Sophie could feel the acidity rising in her voice like bile, filling her throat and making her want to gag. 'Alan was only ever at home in London. The closer he got to here the more he wilted. Do you really think that you're any different? You've bought this wonderful house...' she spread her hands around her to encompass the room '...and thrown yourself into our sleepy little social life, but you won't last long here.'

'Because only dull, boring, timid people can last in a place like this? Aren't you being a little contemptuous of your so-called friends?'

Sophie blushed. 'We grew up here,' she said defensively. Her head was beginning to feel a little woolly, and her thoughts were becoming muddled.

'And I'm an outsider?'

'If you want to put it like that.'

'I see.'

'No, you don't,' Sophie said confusedly. 'I'm not saying that you're not a nice person.' Her jumper was beginning to itch a bit. It was warm in the room, and the drink had made her feel hot and bothered, so, without thinking, she removed it in one easy swoop. 'I'm sure you are, but—'

'I can't possibly be,' Gregory said icily, 'because your husband was successful and he wasn't, and I'm successful so I can't have any redeeming features. Is that your logic?'

'No,' she said, frowning. Was that what she meant? She couldn't think clearly any longer. She stood abruptly and felt dizzy. 'I have to go to bed.'

'Oh, come along,' he said, rising and putting his glass on the side table, 'while you still have control of your legs, woman.'

She didn't want him near her, but he took her arm and she leaned against him. Her legs, now that he had mentioned it, didn't feel altogether supportive.

'Those two drinks seem to have gone straight to my head,' she said apologetically. 'I never drink shorts and I haven't eaten.'

'What do you mean, *you haven't eaten*?' They were heading up the stairs now, very slowly. She had visions of being sick all over his newly laid and very expensive carpet if she moved any more quickly.

'I haven't eaten.'

'When was your last meal?'

Sophie tried to think. 'Whenever. Yesterday some time.'

'Oh, good grief. Aren't you old enough to know how to take care of yourself?'

'It would appear not.'

Underneath her breast his supporting hand burnt through to her skin. Just a fraction higher and he would be able to feel the swell of her soft skin, the tautness of her nipples. Her mind became overwhelmed with the picture of that and she blocked out the thought, dazed by the strength of it.

'And you a sensible librarian and part-time caterer,' he muttered under his breath. In his voice she detected something that made her nerve endings tingle.

'You'll have to use this bedroom,' he said, steering her into a neat, small room, exquisitely furnished in block colours of peach and cream. 'The rest aren't quite finished as yet. It's a bit on the small side, but it should do.'

'Lovely.' She briefly glanced around her and eyed the bed with something approaching hunger. 'Super. Thank you very much. If I could just have a quick lie-down I'll be as right as rain in a few minutes.' She lay down on the bed, which felt deliciously soft and comfortable and warm, and tucked her feet up under her. She could feel her mind drifting away.

Dimly she was aware that Gregory was still in the room, but the effort of forcing her eyes open to confirm the fact was too much effort. Exhaustion. Combined with two strong drinks. She fell asleep.

The next time she woke up the room was still dark, and Gregory was still there. She could hear him shuffling in the background as her head began to clear and her thoughts began to focus.

'I thought you might need these.' He handed her a

glass of water and two aspirin, and she stifled a yawn just long enough to swallow them.

'And this.' He handed her a cup of very sweet tea. She drowsily thought that the man must be a mind-reader, although her head wasn't as bad as she might have expected. More of a dull ache.

'I must have dozed off.' She sat up and had the strangest feeling that something wasn't right, although she wasn't too sure *what*.

'What are you still doing in here anyway?' she said, frowning. Before he could answer she went on, 'Why have you changed?' He was in a pair of light grey trousers and a sweater with broad, football-style stripes across it in grey and cream.

'People tend to when they get up in the morning.' He sat on the side of the bed and stared down at her with dry amusement. Those odd little details which had seemed out of place now began to register slowly on her consciousness, and she stared back at him, aghast.

'Get up in the morning?' she croaked. 'What time is it?'

'A little after nine.'

'What?' She leapt out of bed, horrified. She was immediately and shockingly aware that she was no longer in the clothes she had been wearing when she had climbed onto the bed several hours earlier to close her eyes briefly for what she had thought would be a few minutes. Just until she'd gathered herself together.

'Why didn't you wake me up?' She clutched the over-sized shirt around her body, and she could feel the next question rise unspoken, into the air between them, thickening it and filling it with an undercurrent of horrified awareness.

'Is it still snowing?' she asked, refusing to ask the obvious. Her head no longer hurt but she still felt tired, as though her sleep had been broken during the night. She found that she couldn't look at him without seeing him, in her mind's eye, easing her out of her clothes, removing her bra and replacing her skirt and T-shirt with one of his shirts—without imagining the intimacy of a situation she had slept through. She must have been dead to the world.

'Yes.' She knew that his eyes were fixed on her, even though she had turned her attention to the window and drawn back the curtains to reveal leaden skies, releasing their snowy burden.

'I have to use your telephone,' she said, still with her back to him.

'Why don't you get changed and come downstairs? Your clothes are on the chair by the dressing-table.'

'Yes.' She heard him leave the room silently, closing the door behind him. She raced to it, locked it and frantically began to put on her own things. When she was fully dressed she glanced in the mirror, seeing eyes that were over-bright and cheeks that were burning. With a groan she washed her face vigorously, finger-combed her hair, which was too unruly to do anything with, and nervously made her way downstairs to the kitchen.

He was waiting there for her as he prepared breakfast, whistling under his breath, alarmingly refreshed considering the fact that he had been consuming alcohol steadily the night before and had probably had precious little sleep.

'The telephone's on the dresser.' He stopped whistling to point to the phone and briefly look over his shoulder at her.

'Thank you.' She scuttled across the kitchen with the wariness of someone crossing unknown and mine-ridden territory and called Jade's babysitter, to be told that everything was fine, yes, wasn't the snow just awful, but always the same every year, dear, don't you agree, and, no, don't rush to collect Jade, they were having a fine time.

'I shall have to collect Jade as soon as possible,' she said, replacing the receiver and finally turning her attention to the man standing by the Aga. He's just a man, she told herself, and, worse than that, he's just an Alan Mark 2, but the comparison didn't ring true, and she found her eyes glued to him, reluctantly lingering on the long, lean lines of his body, the width of his shoulders, the chiselled symmetry of his face.

When he turned to her she looked away, embarrassed and confused at her reaction to him.

'I don't think that's advisable at the moment,' he said lazily, motioning for her to sit down and then presenting her with breakfast—toast, marmalade, bacon, eggs, mushrooms.

He sat opposite her at the table and began to tuck into his food, and Sophie hesitantly followed suit. She was, she soon discovered, ravenously hungry. She could have demolished the lot, plate included, in five seconds flat, but she took her time, desperately concentrating on the food in front of her rather than the man sitting opposite.

'I'm awfully sorry that you've found yourself stuck with me here.' She gave a nervous laugh and drank a mouthful of coffee.

'And it's awfully nice of you to be so awfully sorry,' he said, mimicking her.

'There's no need to be sarcastic.'

'You're quite right.' He heaped an undignified amount of mushrooms and bacon onto some toast and consumed the lot in one mouthful. 'But there's no need for you to be so damned polite.'

Sophie didn't say anything. She wasn't going to have an argument with him. It was hardly as though she could storm out of the house if things got too uncomfortable. The snow was showing little sign of letting up, and there was almost no consolation to be had from the thought that snowstorms didn't usually last for too long in these parts. She calmly finished eating, then she stood up, plate in hand, and told him that she would wash the dishes.

'How is Jade?' he asked. He ignored her offer of help, efficiently clearing the kitchen table and positioning himself by the sink. She had the distinct impression that he was irritated with her, for some reason, and she desperately wished that she had had the common sense to make her way back the night before when everyone else had been leaving, instead of insisting on remaining behind to finish doing the job she had been paid to do. All very well and good, being Little Miss Thorough, but just look at where it had landed her.

'Fine.'

He muttered something under his breath. 'Trying to have a conversation with you is like trying to pull teeth,' he told her, and she shrugged as though the remark bothered her not in the slightest.

'Then don't try.'

'And what do you suggest we do?' he asked in a silky voice that made the hairs on the back of her neck stand on end. 'Maintain a frozen silence for as long as you're a prisoner here inside my home?' He had stopped washing and was half-inclined towards her so that he could give her the full benefit of his stare.

He was right. She knew that. She knew that she had to stop being suspicious of every word that left his mouth. She had to stop thinking that the things he said carried some ulterior meaning when he was simply trying to be sociable. The really confusing thing was that she didn't feel like this with anyone else.

She forced herself to look at him and meet his gaze.

'No, that would be silly, wouldn't it?' She continued to dry the dishes and was relieved when he carried on with the washing. 'I guess I'm a little anxious about this snow. Jade isn't accustomed to spending nights away from home.'

'One night,' he corrected. 'Does she not have relatives? Cousins somewhere? Has she never been to stay with them?'

He's not prying, she told herself. 'No.' So what's the harm in letting down a few defences? 'I was an only child and Alan...' He's not an enemy. 'His relations are scattered abroad.' There was cool dismissal in her voice when she said this. 'There's just Jade and me.'

'You came back here because you felt safe here with Jade, didn't you?' he asked gently.

'I suppose so.' She struggled even to admit as much. 'Look.' She carefully dried her hands, placed the tea-towel on the counter and stepped back slightly so that she could meet his eyes, without suffocating in the process. 'I'm not accustomed to...confiding in people. It's nothing to do with you.'

'They say that confession is good for the soul.'

'I shall bear that in mind the next time I'm inside a confessional.'

He smiled crookedly. 'The car will never make it to your place in this weather,' he said, changing the subject, much to her relief, 'so why don't we go and relax and wait for it to stop? If you want to sit in total silence, feel free. I have some work to do, anyway.'

This time they went to a part of the house which she had never been to before—a room at the very end which had been converted into a library of sorts. There were shelves of books, a desk with a computer on top, a filing cabinet in old pine, a couple of chairs and, incongruously, a television perched on one of the shelves.

'You can watch television,' he said, making his way to the desk, 'or read a book, although you might be hard pressed to find any you want to read.' He switched on the computer and sat down. 'Or else...' he glanced at her '...you can just sit and contemplate the vagaries of life.'

'"Contemplate the vagaries of life"? How poetic for someone who builds housing estates.' Sophie sat down, tucked her feet underneath her and didn't look at Gregory, who was fighting to stifle his laughter. 'Why on earth do you have a television in your office?'

'Because,' he said, folding his arms and leaning back in his leather swivel chair, which seemed quite out of keeping, she thought, with the general faded ambience in the room, 'it's useful if I happen to be here late at night and I want to watch the financial news.'

'Or the late night showing of *The Muppets*,' she said, idly picking up the remote control and flicking on the set. 'Will it disturb you if I watch for a few minutes? Probably nothing on but I might get the weather report.'

Gregory didn't answer. He was finding it hard to breathe between muffled gusts of laughter, and Sophie looked at him with concern.

'Are you all right?' she asked, and leaned forward in the chair, hoping that he wasn't having some sort of fit because she wasn't sure if she would be able to handle something like that. She had done a first aid course, but that had been years and years ago. 'Have you choked on something?' She stood up and walked quickly to where he appeared to be doubled over. 'This should do it,' she said vigorously, upon which she administered a hearty slap on his back, and he gave a loud yell of pain.

'What was that for?' His mouth was still twitching, though, and she looked at him narrowly.

'I thought you were choking,' she said, standing back and inspecting him.

'I was laughing.'

'Laughing?'

'Never mind. The moment's gone.' He looked at her and she felt her breath catch in her throat. She couldn't seem to tear her eyes away from his face and her lips remained slightly parted, as though she had been interrupted in the middle of saying something.

'You are quite unlike any woman I have ever met in my life,' he said in an uneven, rough voice, and Sophie could feel embarrassed colour stealing into her cheeks. She couldn't move.

'I'm sure I've heard that cliché somewhere before,' Sophie said, recovering from her momentary confusion. She tilted her head to one side and afforded him a polite, condescending smile. 'Care to tell me how many women you've pulled it out for?'

'Care to tell me why you find it so difficult to accept a compliment?'

He was no longer smiling, and although her moment of disorientation had gone she still felt uneasy.

'Because it's my experience that compliments are usually given with a hidden agenda attached to them.'

'The hidden agenda being…what?'

Sophie went pink and looked away, stubbornly gazing through the window of the study at the snow which, mercifully, appeared to be abating.

'The hidden agenda,' he continued on her behalf, 'being, I take it, that if a man says anything remotely flattering to you then what he's really doing is telling you that he wants to sleep with you. Is that it? Correct me if I'm wrong.'

She dragged her attention away from the wintry scenery outside and met his eyes with steady, cool self-assurance. 'You're absolutely right. I wouldn't have chosen such a basic way of putting it, but you've hit the nail on the head.'

'That's a very jaundiced view of life,' Gregory commented, and she shrugged with an expression of indifference on her face. He could think whatever he pleased about her views on life, her look implied.

'I think the snow's letting up,' she said by way of response, and he glanced briefly at the snow, before returning his eyes to her face.

'I take it your divorce left you with a bitter aftertaste.'

Sophie fixed him with another long, measured look. She didn't care for him nosing into her personal life. The rest of the human race, on the whole, left her alone and that was the way she meant to keep it.

'Spare me your attempts at psychoanalysis, Mr Wallace,' she said, standing up and switching off the television. 'If I ever feel I need help in sorting out my views on life, and I assure you I don't, then I'll pay a professional.'

'I'm not trying to psychoanalyse you,' he told her shortly. 'I may find you vaguely interesting but you haven't as yet entered the category of case study.' He stood up, and she could tell from his face that he was irritated—irritated, she knew, by her lack of response to him. Had he expected her to fall to her knees because he had chosen to pay her a bit of offhand attention? Yes, she thought, he probably had.

'I'm relieved to hear it,' Sophie said without bothering to camouflage the edge of sarcasm in her voice. 'I'll cancel my appointment with the shrink forthwith!' She smiled brightly at him and then reminded him that she really would like to leave before the snow had a change of heart and recommenced its onslaught on the landscape. 'Jade will start worrying,' she said truthfully, and he gave a brief nod.

Even with her coat on, it was freezing outside. The path had to be cleared, which meant shovelling away snow for forty-five minutes, but after that things weren't as difficult as she had anticipated. Her fingers were raw, though, when she was finally seated next to him in the Range Rover, and she rubbed her hands together briskly to get the circulation flowing.

'I think I have hypothermia in my fingers,' she said, holding them out and inspecting them.

'I told you that you needn't help,' he grated, revving the engine and slowly manoeuvring the car out down the long drive and towards the road.

'I know.'

'But you insisted, to prove…what? Your independence?' he asked mildly, and she shot him a smouldering, sidelong look.

'Why on earth should I let you do it all yourself?' she asked flatly. 'If it hadn't been for me, you wouldn't be in this car now, having to make your way to my house. Besides, independence has nothing to do with it. In these parts of the world—'

'Oh, good grief,' he said. 'Anyone would think that this was a small village in the remotest part of Siberia.'

She felt a grin surface and controlled it, then it surfaced again.

'Women here…shovel snow in winter!' she said brightly. 'In Knightsbridge they have themselves manicured; in Ashdown, shovelling snow is the next best thing. Besides, in case you hadn't noticed, I'm built for snow shovelling.'

She wished she hadn't said that because he flicked his eyes across to her, a fleeting inspection, before he looked ahead of him.

'I wouldn't put it quite that way,' he said with a shadow of a smile, and she felt herself go a ferocious red. 'Arm-wresting, perhaps...'

'Oh, ha, ha, very funny. You need to turn next right.'

They drove in silence for a while. At the babysitter's house she collected Jade and her various belongings, anxious to be on her way. She declined Ann's offer of a cup of tea and ignored the curiosity on her face as she took in the driver behind the wheel of the car. There was a flurry of grateful thank-yous for having Jade for the night, then the short trip back to their home.

'So,' Gregory said, when he finally pulled up outside the house, 'would you like to invite me in for a cup of tea?'

Sophie opened the car door and began to help Jade with her things, slinging her bag over one shoulder.

'I would, but I have a million things to do.'

'Ah, yes, the housework...'

'That's right. It never ends.' She stepped out of the car and then half lifted Jade out from behind. 'Thank you very much for putting me up, and for giving me a lift back. As soon as this weather clears I'll come and fetch my car.' She shut the car door and was on the verge of moving off when she saw the window roll down.

'I'll be seeing you around,' he said, looking at her with one hand on the steering-wheel and the other on the gear lever.

'Possibly. It's a small place.'

Before he could embark on anything resembling a conversation she turned away, holding Jade's hand, and headed towards the front door. She could feel his eyes on her back as she fumbled in her bag for the key.

Maybe it was the bracing weather, or maybe just the heralding of a new year, but Sophie hadn't felt this alive in a long time.

CHAPTER SIX

'THAT,' Sophie said to Kat, stirring sugar into her tea and tentatively taking a sip, 'is absolutely the one thing I can't stand.'

They were in the now completely refurbished hotel, having lunch. Toasted sandwiches. Aside from the renovations, the menu, Sophie noticed, appeared to have changed as well. There were all sorts of interesting things on it now. The sandwiches were no longer the basic choices of ham, cheese, roast beef or egg. The Farringdons had clearly done some research into Light Snacks and had pushed the boat out with avocado, curried chicken and cheeses other than the staple Cheddar, as well as all manner of other things. Malcolm had clearly heard the rumours of another hotel going up, and was attempting to rope in his regulars just in case.

'It's never bothered you before,' Kat pointed out reasonably.

'Well, it bothers me now,' Sophie replied with a touch of pique in her voice. 'The entire village seems to know that I spent a night—*one night*—at that man's house. If they're not asking me what it's like inside, they're looking at me as though I'm hiding a guilty secret.'

'Which, of course, you're not.'

'Which, of course, I most *certainly* am not!' Sophie responded hotly. She gestured for the bill and glared at her friend. 'I only stayed there because I couldn't leave! The choice was either freeze to death, trying to make a getaway, or spend one night there. What would you have done!'

'Have I said anything?' Kat asked innocently. 'It's hardly my fault that gossip spreads fast in our wee little village. Besides, if *I* had to have a rumour circulating around me and a man, I can't think of a dishier one than Gregory Wallace!'

'I thought you were seeing the man-under-the-mistletoe,' Sophie said, allowing herself to be distracted, and Kat grinned.

'Oh, yes! Mark. Adorable, but rather more humdrum than the sexy Mr Wallace. Then again, I *am* of the common garden variety.' She eyed her friend with a raised eyebrow and an expression that said, unlike you.

That struck Sophie as being particularly unfair, seeing that she made no effort whatsoever to upgrade her appearance.

Still, she thought as she headed back to the library, it had relieved some of her irritation to talk to Kat. She also had to admit that her friend had been perfectly correct: she had never minded the smallness of Ashdown village. Indeed, she had always liked it—enjoyed the way it wrapped around her like a security blanket.

She had no intention of getting herself into any sort of situation with the man again, and in time all those good-natured rumours would fizzle out.

The thought of that bucked her up until, just as she was about to shut up the library for the day, she looked up and saw Gregory, walking through the door towards her. Immediately she could feel the tension seep into her body, as though through an invisible drip. Why on earth did he have this exasperating effect on her?

She waited until he was standing in front of her, and then she said, 'You certainly make a habit of bad timing, don't you?'

'Just coming to return my book,' he told her, produc-

ing the book with a flourish. 'I felt so intimidated by the
prospect of a fine that I read it in double quick time!'

'Here. I'll take it.' She held out her hand and eyed
him with impatience when he continued to hold the book
aloft.

'I'll hand it over if you agree to come out to dinner
with me.'

Sophie bent over, collected her handbag and smiled
at him politely. 'In that case, you can come back tomorrow and hand it to Claire.'

He dropped the book on the counter, as she'd known
he would, and she efficiently logged it in and slipped on
her coat.

'So,' he said, falling into step alongside her, 'what
about dinner?'

'What about it?' she replied, briskly walking towards
the door. She opened it, stood aside to let him out and
then locked it behind her. With her luck, she thought
glumly, Malcolm in the hotel across the road would just
happen to be passing by one of the windows and another
rumour would be added to the pile.

'Must you act so threatened by a simple invitation for
a meal?'

She turned to face him, even though she could hardly
make out his face under the half-hearted glow of the
streetlights. 'I am not in the running for dinner invitations, Mr Wallace...'

'Gregory...'

'Whatever. I thought I had made myself clear to you
before.'

He leaned leisurely against the lamppost. 'I understand you're quite involved in fund-raising on behalf of
handicapped children.'

'Yes...' She looked at him warily, wondering where
this line of chitchat was leading.

'I'd like to make a sizeable donation,' he told her. 'And before you launch into a speech about blackmail let me just add that I make a sizeable donation to various charities every year. It's purely coincidental that when I mentioned in passing to someone that I was interested in a local charity I was pointed in your direction.'

Sophie found herself stuck for a suitable response, and in the ensuing silence he continued with relentless logic, 'If we meet for dinner we could discuss this further. It would be nice to know how the money would be distributed.'

Defeated, she sighed with exasperation because, despite his cool-headed rationale, she felt as though she had been cunningly ambushed. 'Oh, very well.'

'Tomorrow night?'

'I suppose so.'

'Don't for goodness' sake, sound so thrilled.'

She ignored that. 'But it'll have to be at my house. There are enough rumours doing the rounds about—'

'Ah, yes. Those rumours.' There was amusement in his voice. 'Annoying, aren't they?' He didn't sound in the least annoyed. He sounded highly entertained. 'That's fine. I'll drop by your place some time around eight tomorrow evening?'

'Fine.'

That, Sophie thought despondently that night, was the last thing she wanted. Having persuaded herself that her contact with the man would now be solely of the happened-to-meet-in-the-street variety, here she was, facing a dinner *à deux*.

She found that she could hardly concentrate the following day. She spent some time gathering together all the relevant facts about the charity, but every few seconds—or so it seemed—her mind would flit ahead to the evening, and resolutely stick with the image.

She did her shopping in the afternoon, and then cooked a simple pasta meal, which she reckoned would have the added bonus of being quick to eat.

Jade, having been allowed some leeway in helping, viewed this as an opening to branch out on some experimental cooking of her own, and at seven-thirty Sophie found herself pulling out a cake from the Aga. As she had expected, Jade had conveniently gone to bed, which left her to ice the thing. That, in turn, gave her approximately twenty minutes to change.

By the time eight o'clock rolled around she was still in the process of trying to tame her hair into something respectable.

She heard the doorbell ring a few times, and when eventually she ran to open it she found Gregory on the doorstep, impatiently consulting his watch.

'Sorry,' she said, stepping aside to let him in. 'Running late.'

'I was beginning to think that you'd decided to stand me up,' he told her, brushing past her into the small hallway.

'Did you imagine that I was cowering under the bed with some ear plugs in?' Sophie asked dryly. 'That would have been a rather foolish ploy, don't you think?'

'Well, you're so utterly unpredictable that I have no idea what to expect from you.' He removed his coat, which she took from him and slung casually over the banister. He was wearing dark trousers and a black, loosely knitted jumper. She stood back, eyed him critically and said, 'You look like a cat burglar.'

'Merely trying to make sure that I was camouflaged under cover of darkness,' he replied with exaggerated seriousness. 'You never know who's pulling back the net curtains and spying on your house to see what's going on. I wouldn't want to be responsible for yet more rumours, sullying your virtuous reputation.

'I doubt that my reputation is something you lose sleep about,' Sophie answered, moving towards the sitting room, very much aware of his presence behind her.

'And I'm surprised that all those rumours bother you at all,' he responded. 'You don't strike me as the sort who worries too much about what other people think.'

Sophie wondered whether this was something he had deduced from the way she dressed—because she didn't conform to the stereotyped image of sexy clothes designed to impress. Tonight's fascinating ensemble was a black and red gypsy-style skirt virtually down to her ankles and a long-sleeved, loose-fitting black silk shirt which she wore over it. The lace-up boots, her favourites, were unfortunately really only suitable for outdoor wear. Instead, she was clad in flat, black, rather sensible loafers. Her hair, which refused to be manoeuvred into anything chic, had been tied back in a long braid, with sufficient loose strands to cast doubt on the hairdo.

'I don't,' she said bluntly, gesturing to a chair and watching as he sat down. She remained standing in front of him and folded her arms. 'I do, however, prefer people to have the correct impression of me.'

'In other words, if we had spent a night of passion you wouldn't give it a second thought.' He looked straight at her when he said this, and although she felt a little bit unnerved by his stare she refused to let it throw her into a state of confusion. Alan, she remembered, had used the very same tactics to bowl her over. Gregory was not playing the same game, but she was no fool. She knew that it was very easy to be ambushed by a certain brand of charm, without even realising it.

'Would you like something to drink?' she asked pleasantly, sidestepping his question. 'I don't have much by way of choice. Wine, white or red, whisky, possibly gin.'

'A glass of white wine would be nice,' he said, and she vanished in the direction of the kitchen, returning with two glasses of wine. A short, polite preamble, a quick dinner and some of Jade's cake. The entire evening could be wrapped up in under two hours.

'Now,' she said, sitting opposite him and producing the literature she had gathered from where she had placed it on the table next to her chair, 'I've got some information here on the charity, as well as the accounts…' She leaned forward and he obediently took the paperwork from her. 'Perhaps you would care to have a flick through, then you can ask me any questions you have.'

'How businesslike of you,' he murmured. He gave everything a cursory glance and deposited the lot on the table in front of him. 'That looks fine.' He then proceeded to tell her how much he intended to contribute, and she had to control the urge to choke on her mouthful of wine.

'That's very generous. Thank you.'

'I'm a very generous person. And you're welcome.' He sat back, extended his arm along the back of the chair and crossed his legs. 'Now, tell me why you decided to get into charity work.'

He hadn't even made much of a pretence of looking through the things she had collated for him. He had scanned a few bits, but in a rudimentary fashion. Did he now think that he would devote the remainder of the evening to trying to prise her open? Why? Why would he even want to bother when she had given him no encouragement whatsoever? Just the opposite, in fact.

She knew why, of course, and her mouth tightened. It was nothing to do with *her*. It was all verbal foreplay, designed to get her into bed. She had felt his interest almost from the very beginning, and she suspected that her polite lack of response had whetted his appetite. When a man could have any woman he wanted, he really felt the challenge of the woman who didn't want him.

There was no vanity in this deduction, no warm feeling of flattery that Gregory Wallace, most wanted man in town, had temporarily focused his attention in her direction. He must, she thought, be totally blind if he couldn't see that her defences, in full working order, made her immune to him.

'I thought you were interested in seeing where your money was going to go,' she said coolly. 'You've barely scanned the stuff on the table.'

'I trust you,' he said lazily, eyeing her over the rim of his glass as he slowly savoured a mouthful of wine. 'Is there any reason why I shouldn't?'

'In which case you could have posted me your cheque and left me to get on with it.'

'I could have.' He shrugged. 'But has it occurred to you that I might want to get to know you?'

'No.' *Get to know her?* That had a familiar ring to it. 'Are you ready to eat?' She drained her glass, stood up and looked at him. 'Do you like pasta?'

'I love it.' Gregory got to his feet, and she could tell from the expression on his face that he was slightly annoyed. Then, without warning, another wayward thought sprang into her head—the thought of that night, of his hands on her as he'd undressed her, without her even realising it. For a split instant she wondered what it would feel like to be undressed by him and to be aware of the experience, to have his hands caress her body.

Sophie turned away abruptly and began to head towards the kitchen, angry with herself for the way her mind had temporarily lapsed.

The table in the kitchen was already laid, and she heated the food, then served them both. Pasta, garlic bread, salad. Then she sat down and gestured to him to eat.

Gradually she began to relax. His conversation, she found, when he wasn't trying to get inside her mind, was vastly interesting. He was one of those men, she quickly realised, who could converse on almost any topic under the sun—art, literature, economics, anything. When she remarked on this he told her with amusement that he wasn't just a builder. He had left behind a thriving publishing business in New York, and much of his personal investments were in paintings.

'And you donate large sums of money to charities,' Sophie said, twirling spaghetti round her fork and looking at him. 'A sensitive, intellectual builder with a caring nature. Where does it end? Do you speak twelve languages as well? I'm impressed.'

'No, you're not,' he corrected her a little acidly. He sat back, pushing his chair a little way from the table so that he could cross his legs. He surveyed her thoughtfully as she finished eating and placed her fork and spoon on her plate. 'You're far too bitter to be impressed by anyone.'

'Oh, observer of human nature as well. I'll just add that to the list.' She stood up, a little put out by his blunt analysis, and stretched over to reach his plate.

'Sit down,' he said, flicking out his hand and grasping her by her wrist. The feel of his fingers against her skin brought her to a momentary standstill. Everything in her body seemed to slow down for an instant. Then the beating of her heart and the race of her pulse went into overdrive, and she had to concentrate very hard on keeping her wits about her. It was a very strange sensation— very frightening because nothing like this had happened to her in a long time. She had become so accustomed to controlling situations that to find herself in a situation that threatened to control her threw her into a state of panic.

'I told you,' she said coldly, 'I don't like my space being invaded.' She could hear her heart hammering away inside her, like the rapid, steady beat of a drum.

'I'm not invading your space,' he said softly. 'I am trying to have a conversation.'

They stared at one another for a short space of time, and Sophie lowered her eyes. When she sat down again—because it was frankly easier than remaining on her feet—she found that she was trembling. She poured herself another glass of wine to steady her nerves, and took a few deep sips from it.

'What do you think of the housing estate?' he asked, and she breathed a sigh of relief because she was fine when it came to conversing on neutral topics.

'Better than I thought it was going to be,' she admitted, not quite looking at him but still acutely aware of his masculine magnetism. Black suited him. It emphasised that aura of rakishness that he exuded. There was something dark and exciting and vaguely dangerous about him. Was he aware of that? He must be, she thought. Alan had always been keenly aware of his personal appeal, although his appeal had been far more urbane. He hadn't possessed Gregory's immediate, primitive impact, but he had always made up for that with his polish and surface charm.

She sipped some more of her wine, then finished off what was in her glass and poured herself another. The clear, cold liquid fortified her.

'We were all horrified when we heard about it,' she expanded, playing with the stem of her glass. 'We imagined that our little village would find itself on the outskirts of a concrete jungle so, yes, what can I say? You're a good builder.'

Gregory laughed. 'I don't actually lay the bricks myself,' he told her wryly. 'I merely own the construction firm.'

'But you must have had some say in what went up.'

'Naturally.'

'In which case, you're a good...whatever...judge of property development. I don't know very much about the construction business.' She tilted her head to one side. 'You could always fill me in. I gather men like talking about their little pet joys.'

'I am constantly amazed at your mastery of the English language,' he replied, linking his fingers together loosely on his lap and staring at her. She really wished that he wouldn't do that. Her head was beginning to feel fuzzy enough without those hypnotic eyes on her. 'And I wouldn't dream of boring you with details of what I do for a living. What did your husband do?'

He dropped his eyes when he said this, and although somewhere inside her she knew that she should resent his question she found herself saying, 'He was in business. Finance. He worked for one of the big finance houses in the City.' She gave a short, acid laugh. She drank a little more of her wine and then proceeded to stare at the glass. Alan had liked money. He had liked earning huge amounts, and he had enjoyed the privileges that came with living in the fast lane—the open top sports car, the penthouse in Knightsbridge, the weekends in five-star hotels in Europe.

Was it any surprise that her initial reservations about him had been swept aside by his relentless, determined courtship? Although she hadn't been immediately bowled over by him physically, she had acknowledged that he was an attractive man, and his persistent bombardment of flowers and chocolates, imported specially from Belgium, had eventually won her over. She had spent her whole life in the sheltered community of Ashdown and then, suddenly, there she was, adored by a man who showered her with things she had never even dreamt of.

She finished another glass of wine. Her second? Third? And she heard herself open up haltingly.

'He came from a very working-class background.' She addressed the wine glass. Her words seemed to be coming from a long way off—from another person, in fact. Not from Sophie Turner who kept herself to herself and never confided in anyone. Not from the Sophie Turner who had spent so many years constructing walls around her that her ability to open up had been lost.

'He used to say that when he was a child he would see people driving around in their big cars in their expensive suits, and he always knew that one day he would be one of them.' She began to pour herself another glass of wine and then thought better of it. At this rate she wouldn't be able to make it up the stairs, and with a child in the house there was no way that a hangover was a good idea. Children and hangovers didn't go together.

'That's not an unusual reaction,' Gregory commented, which reminded her that she was talking to him. Of all people. She tried to gather herself together and retreat back into her fortress, but failed.

'Alan was never going to settle for second best.' She resumed her far-away conversation with her glass. 'In fact, he loathed the middle ground. He wanted everything, and he succeeded. He was basically very brash, very pushy, but he learnt to turn those qualities into charm and the right sort of aggression to get ahead.'

'How did you meet?'

'I did some catering for his company. He spotted me

instantly. My looks, you see…' She grimaced. 'He liked the colour of my hair and my height. He thought I looked dramatic. Just the right sort of person to hang on his arm. And, of course, I was young. Young enough to mould into what he wanted.'

'And what did he want?' Gregory asked with mild curiosity.

'He wanted…someone who was prepared to live in his shadow. He bought my clothes for me, chose them himself. He had a fear of my country gaucheness coming out.' She sighed and stood up. As she did so it occurred to her that she really had drunk a bit too much because her feet felt unsteady and she had to take a deep breath, before leaning over for Gregory's plate. This time he didn't reach out to pull her back down. He allowed her to clear the table, then he rescued a teatowel, which was hanging precariously half off the kitchen counter, and stood next to her at the sink.

'There's no need for you to help,' Sophie told him. 'I shall leave all this until tomorrow evening.'

'Nonsense, we might as well clear it all now.'

Sophie shrugged and began to wash the dishes. When she was finished she looked around her and then said that there was some cake to be eaten.

'Chocolate,' she said, producing the item in question from the larder. Now that she was moving about she felt a bit better. 'Jade loves baking.' She smiled, without concealing her delight, when she thought of her daughter. 'Or rather she just loves measuring things and mixing the ingredients together. I'm afraid when she comes down in the morning she'll be quite crestfallen if a sizeable amount hasn't been eaten.'

'In that case, I'll have a very large slice,' Gregory told her obligingly.

'You needn't force yourself.' She glanced at him with

the cake slice in her hand, and not for the first time was vaguely confused by that curious mix of emotions he produced in her—threatened, wary, suspicious, and yet, underneath all those feelings, a stirring of excitement, a curious sensation of being utterly and completely alive for the first time in her life.

'I happen to like chocolate cake,' he told her dryly, 'especially ones shaped like teddy bears.'

'Yes, well…' She cut him a generous slab, made them both a cup of coffee and led the way to the sitting room. Kitchen chairs were no good for curling up in, and she felt as though she needed to tuck herself into a comfortable chair.

'How does your daughter fare at school?' he asked conversationally as they both sat down.

'Why do you ask?' Sophie said, looking at him narrowly.

'Oh, sorry. I forgot that asking you personal questions was an affront.'

Somehow he managed to make her reticence on something that was perfectly innocent sound like churlishness. How did he do that?

She couldn't believe that she had spoken to him at length—or what was for her at length—about Alan. Was it because she had had a little to drink and the alcohol had loosened her tongue. Or had some weird form of nervousness catapulted her into gabbling? Or had his complete lack of judgemental attitude on what she had said encouraged her to elaborate when she would ordinarily have held back?

She didn't know. What she did know, however, was that the inclination to open up to him made her uneasy.

'Shall we change the subject?' he asked, when she still hadn't replied. 'Perhaps we could talk a bit about the weather. Or the roadworks taking place just outside the village. Nice, safe topics that don't throw you into a tizzy.'

'Your questions do not throw me into a tizzy,' Sophie said indignantly.

'Oh, my mistake.'

'Jade, if you're *really* interested, does very well at school. She's in the top three, as a matter of fact.' She couldn't resist a proud smile at this. 'Her deafness may be a handicap, but it certainly hasn't been an impediment. She's a quick learner and she's fortunate in so far as all the teachers have been wonderful. Patient.' She looked away quickly because she could feel tears coming to her eyes.

It had been a long, hard struggle when her daughter was born, facing a future that had seemed uncertain at the time. More than at any other time Sophie had longed for the support of a husband, a good, caring, strong husband who could help take the weight and responsibility from her shoulders now and again.

'Perhaps I should leave,' Gregory said gently.

'Yes! No. I don't know.' She laughed uncertainly. 'Well, at least finish your coffee. The charity,' she continued hurriedly, 'is having a function in the village hall in a week's time. I'm sure it's not your cup of tea, but you're welcome to come along.' She couldn't believe that she was actually inviting this man to something when she had resolutely told herself that she would make sure to avoid him at all costs. Then she reminded herself that he was now a benefactor. She hung onto this reasoning and felt a great deal calmer.

'Some of the ladies in the village are going to be selling their crafts,' she said in a businesslike tone of voice. 'I don't suppose you'll be interested in stuffed toys... Have you any nieces? Nephews?'

'No. I was an only child.'

'Well…lots of hand-knitted stuff as well. Decorations. You know. That sort of thing.'

'Sounds interesting.' He stood up, and now that he appeared to be leaving she felt an overwhelming sense of disappointment.

'I'm sure you don't really think so,' she said stiffly, regretting the invitation. What on earth would a man like Gregory Wallace be doing at a local fund-raising craft fair in a village hall? 'But it's kind of you to say so.'

'Oh, for goodness' sake!' He moved across to where she was still sitting with her feet curled underneath her, and leaned over with his hands on either arm of her chair. 'Will you stop typecasting me as the big, bad wolf?'

'I was doing no such thing,' Sophie protested. She pressed herself back in the chair. His nearness made her feel claustrophobic.

'You damn well were. Every time you take a tiny step out of that ivory tower of yours to test the water you retreat, as though you're scared stiff that you might just end up letting down some of your defences.'

'Stop trying to analyse me!' She could hardly breathe now. More than his words, his presence was having an effect on her, making her addled.

He sighed with frustration and straightened. 'Well, are you going to see me to the door?'

Sophie rose, not bothering to put her shoes back on. She walked with him slowly out into the small hallway, watching as he slung on his coat. Then he turned to face her, raking his fingers through his hair, then stuck his hands in the pockets of his coat.

'Thank you for a very…interesting evening,' he said, with something approaching a smile. 'Delicious food. Do you get much call for catering in these parts?'

'Enough for it to remain at the level of a hobby.'

'You really should broaden your net,' he said politely.

'I haven't the time. There's my charity work and the library. And, of course, Jade.' She moved towards the door and rested her hand lightly on the doorknob. 'Thanks again for your contribution. It was very kind of you.'

'And on that terribly courteous note, shall I take my leave?' His voice was cutting, and for reasons she could hardly identify she felt hurt. What had he expected of the evening? she wondered.

'Drive safely.'

'And, no doubt, you'll see me around. Is that it? If, of course, you don't manage to scurry away into a convenient doorway so you can avoid the tedium of talking to me.' He gave her a hard, cool look and she felt the colour crawl into her cheeks.

His accusations were justified, and she couldn't think of anything to say by way of response—largely because she had never found herself in a situation like this before. She was certain that the few men in the past who had approached her on some of her rare excursions into public life had felt similarly put out by her lack of response, but they had never said anything. They had simply slunk away.

Gregory Wallace, though, was of a different breed. He was a man who spoke his mind. He wasn't afraid of her sharp tongue and he had no time for her defensive reticence whenever it came to speaking about herself.

'You're welcome to believe what you want to believe,' she told him eventually, folding her arms and meeting his eyes with stubborn defensiveness.

'Yes, well, it's much easier for you to adopt that attitude, isn't it?'

'What do you mean?'

'That way you can hide for ever from the real world outside your front door.'

'I'm not hiding from anything!'

'Oh, yes, you are.'

'What gives you the right to…to…make statements like that?' Sophie spluttered, angry and confused. 'Is it so difficult to just accept that I'm not interested in you?'

'You're not interested in anything or anyone who threatens to throw you back into society.'

'Well, Gregory, you can think what you like…' It was the first time she had used his name and the sudden, ridiculous intimacy she felt at this plunged her into further confusion.

'Yes, I can. And do. And,' he added softly, 'in turn I'll give you something to think about.'

His lips touched hers before she even realised what he was going to do. She felt his mouth against hers and in a moment of sheer, bewildering, overpowering desire she returned his kiss—fiercely, hungrily, passionately. His tongue, probing hers, was shockingly erotic and she closed her eyes, savouring the taste and feel of him.

But almost as suddenly her body went numb with shock. There was a moment of frozen horror then she pulled back, trembling.

'Please leave,' she whispered.

'Before the outside world becomes too tantalising?' he said harshly.

'You flatter yourself!'

'Do you really believe that?'

The question dropped between them and hung there in agonising silence before he turned away and let himself out, slamming the door behind him. Which left her alone with her thoughts—a whirlwind of chaotic emotions which was so frightening in its potency that she remained where she was for a few minutes, unable to move, her head resting against the closed door.

She didn't want this. She wanted her calm, uneventful, vaguely unfulfilled life back because the alternative, now looming menacingly on the horizon, wasn't worth thinking about.

CHAPTER SEVEN

THE weather turned out to be just perfect for the craft fair—cold, but blindingly sunny. There would be a good turn-out. Everyone in the charity group had worked hard, and Sophie did her very best to be enthusiastic, but as she arranged stalls, occasionally looking around her to make sure that Jade had not strayed out of the large room, her mind was depressingly occupied with thoughts of Gregory Wallace.

She had let him kiss her. Worse, she had enjoyed it. Her body, frozen for years, had betrayed her. Two minutes of unthinking, sensual pleasure had caused a succession of sleepless nights.

On the one hand, she argued with herself, a simple kiss was hardly a portent of approaching personal disaster. In fact, she told herself, it would have been unnatural if she had managed to spend the rest of her life completely divorced from the opposite sex.

Gregory Wallace, when she thought about it, had done her a favour because in a strange way he was just the right sort of man to awaken that temporary breach of self-control simply because he was so utterly *wrong*. She could kiss him, safe in the knowledge that nothing would ever come of it because she was innately too suspicious of men of his ilk.

For five minutes the internal debate made sense. Then the creeping uneasiness stole over her again. She remembered how she'd felt the precise moment his mouth had touched hers, and the memory sent her into a state of barely concealed panic.

116

She tried to remember how she had felt with Alan. She decided that if she could only hold onto those bad memories they would protect her, but Alan, having managed so successfully to ruin her hopes and dreams, now seemed to be too blurry a figure to grasp.

What had she felt for him? In retrospect she wondered whether it had ever been love. His persistence had eventually won her over, but their entire life had been lived in the public arena. Had there been any moments of true closeness? Had they laughed together? Shared jokes? She dubiously supposed that they must have done, but nagging at the back of her mind was the suspicion that she had simply been bowled over and, having married him, had dutifully persevered in a pact which she'd believed should not be broken.

She finished arranging her stand, and stood back to look at it. The patchwork cushions, elaborately worked by Mrs Wilson, the oldest member of the group, were the pièces de résistance, and she had stuck those at the front. The effect, discernible to her but not, she hoped, to other people, was a staggered affair, with the most amateurish efforts at the very back.

She glanced around the room, and was generally pleased with the rest of the stalls, which ranged from intricately knitted children's clothes to bric-à-brac. Most of the assorted paraphernalia she wouldn't have dreamt of putting in her own home, but already there were lots of new faces milling around, people from the newly built housing estate, and doubtless they would find the stuff appealing. Authentic country fare, she supposed.

Jade was playing in the far corner of the room with two girls in her class. Sophie waved, smiling, then she slipped back behind her stall, satisfied that they would raise a tidy sum for their efforts, despite the time of year.

Kat, who'd had to be forcibly persuaded into helping

out, was casting a jaundiced eye around the room. She had made a mug of coffee for Sophie and she handed it to her.

'Honestly, Soph, can't you try and get your group to knit a few more trendy things for kids?'

'This is Ashdown, Kat. Not Camden Lock. Parents like the old-fashioned knitted clothes.' As if to order, they looked across to Gloria Newson's stall to see two old dears, making appreciative noises over two little cardigans.

'Ah! But what about the children? Do *they* like designs that went out with the ark?'

'Don't be horrible.' But Sophie was grinning.

'There's so much scope for fashionable knitwear! Miniskirts for teenagers! Cropped tops…short dresses. How many models do you ever see sporting chunky cardies with those great, unappealing brown buttons?'

She carried on grousing in the background while people came and went, buying bits and pieces. The regulars tut-tutted in their usual fashion at the prices, which were ridiculously low, but a lot of the newcomers snapped up the stuff with the enthusiasm of people who knew they were getting bargains.

'I shall have to think about raising the prices next time around,' Sophie said, as over the course of the morning the contents of her stall depleted rapidly.

Kat snorted. 'The faithfuls won't appreciate that!'

'True, but inflation…' Sophie shrugged. 'The times, they are a-changing…' She sighed, grinning and shaking her head in a rueful manner.

'Aren't they just?' Kat, looking past Sophie, narrowed her eyes tellingly. 'And through the door has just stepped one of those fine examples of our changing times. Now what do you imagine *he's* doing here? Don't tell me that he's shopping for bargains for his country house!'

Sophie turned around, her hands still clasping her mug. She knew who had just entered, without his name having to be mentioned.

As usual, Gregory was attracting his fair share of side-long glances, even though his face was now well known in the village. As he moved slowly through the hall he stopped at each stall and inspected things with interest, asking questions.

Sophie, who had managed successfully to put him to the back of her mind, felt an awakening of butterflies in her stomach. Thank heavens Kat wasn't looking at her. She was probably the only person who would have been able to sense her agitation.

He spotted Jade, and Sophie watched with a tightening stomach as he went across to her. He stooped and spoke to her, saying something funny to judge from the expression on Jade's face and making the little girls giggle as he inspected their collection of dolls.

When he straightened Sophie looked away quickly, loath to be caught looking at him. Kat was not quite so discreet. She continued with a minute-by-minute commentary on his progress through the hall, which she interspersed with exclamations of curiosity as to what on earth would have brought him to a village fair of all things.

'You're getting repetitive,' Sophie said eventually. 'Who knows why the man's here? *Who cares?*'

Kat swivelled to scrutinise her friend's face. 'Maybe he's come to catch a glimpse of the elusive fair Sophie,' she said in a dramatic whisper, and Sophie, irritated, felt the colour rise into her face.

'Your imagination's breaking free from its leash again, Kat.' Her voice was steady and amused, but she felt dizzy and her head seemed suddenly to be stuffed with cotton wool.

'Yes…' Kat carried on, inclining her head away, 'and as he moves through the room he cuts a dashing figure in his deep green trousers and thick, chunky, oatmeal jumper—fortunately, no unappealing brown buttons in sight—with his coat casually draped over one arm. Yes…and he's stopping to have a chat with Mrs Godfrey, who appears to be responding coyly to whatever he's saying… Clearly he's not telling her that she needs to go on an immediate weight reduction programme, and he's moving on…'

'Shut up, Kat!' But Sophie was giggling and trying hard to keep a straight face.

'It would seem that he's coming in this direction!' Kat spun around. 'Now, Soph, could we *do* something with that hair of yours, darling?' She began to arrange Sophie's hair, while Sophie made frantic, slapping motions with her hands.

In the middle of this Gregory said, with amusement in his voice. 'This is uncharacteristically buoyant behaviour for two responsible stall-holders.'

Not meeting his eye, Sophie smoothed her hair away from her face.

'Sophie *can* be a trifle high-spirited,' Kat said, grinning broadly. 'Usually a sign that she's getting a little restless.'

'Is that a fact?' Gregory looked at Sophie for longer than was necessary. 'I shall bear that in mind.'

'How nice of you to come,' Sophie said, ignoring Kat's infectiously smiling face and doing her best to look composed. 'What do you think of our little craft fair?' The stiff breeze outside had tousled his hair, giving him a disarmingly sexy appearance.

'Very impressive.' He looked at Sophie and she felt her skin begin to glow. 'And very successful from the looks of it.'

'Yes, there are more people than we expected, as a matter of fact. Must have something to do with that housing estate of yours.' Kat frowned at her and she blushed, embarrassed at the brusqueness in her voice. 'That very attractive housing estate,' she amended, which only made it sound worse. 'Lots of people looking for bargains for their new homes,' she ended feebly.

'And how is *your* new home coming along?' Kat chipped in with her usual brand of effervescent enthusiasm.

'You should both come along some time and have a look for yourselves,' Gregory said politely. Even though he was addressing her friend, Sophie could feel his attention on her. Her body was responding to the knowledge, though the response was something she neither invited nor wanted.

'Doesn't that sound like fun, Soph?'

'Oh, absolutely,' Sophie said politely. 'I can hardly contain myself.' She hadn't meant to say that. The words emerged almost involuntarily and she gave a little sigh of inward frustration.

His effect on her was appalling. There was no escaping the fact. With the rest of the human race she was the epitome of self-control, a model of rectitude. The minute he was around all those qualities went into hiding, and she was jumpy, nervous and reduced to defensive, childish outbursts which made her cringe inside.

'Sophie!' Kat hissed at her under her breath.

'Why bother?' Gregory said coolly. 'Does your friend ever take advice from anyone?'

'She *can* be a little headstrong,' Kat responded awkwardly, sensing an atmosphere.

'Oh, for goodness sake, you two,' Sophie muttered impatiently. 'Could you save it for when I'm not around?' She turned away abruptly and left the stall, walking quickly towards Jade so that she could start gathering her dolls together and getting ready to leave.

Most of the contents of the stalls had been sold, and the remainder were now being packed away into boxes to go back to the charity shop. In the background she could hear stragglers, making arrangements for lunch. She didn't know whether Gregory was still standing at her stall, chatting to Kat, and she told herself that she didn't care. He was still here, fingering a tea-cosy, of all things.

Sophie looked at him. 'Are you interested in buying it?' she asked. 'Because if you're not I'd like to pack it away.'

He handed it to her and she turned away from him, arranging her boxes, of which there were only two remaining, and collating her tin of money.

'How would you two like to have lunch with me?' she heard him ask from behind her, and she paused for a moment in what she was doing.

From behind her, Kat said wistfully that she would love to but she had to get back to work.

'What about you?' Gregory addressed Sophie's back. 'You and Jade, that is…'

'I'm afraid I really can't.' Sophie turned reluctantly. 'I must go to the market as soon as I've finished here…'

'Is that the one in the square?'

'Yes.' She beckoned to Jade, who reluctantly left her friends and began to meander in their direction. 'Hurry up!' Sophie mouthed, and Jade hastened her steps by a fraction.

'In that case, I'll join you. I've been meaning to go along there for a while.' He looked at her implacably, and out of the corner of her eye she could see Kat gazing at her, round-eyed.

'I…' Sophie began, cornered.

'Great market!' Kat said encouragingly to Gregory.

'You must go. Lovely fruit and veg, all home-grown, of course. I need some carrots,' she said to Sophie.

Before Sophie could reply Gregory said firmly, 'I'll make sure that she remembers to get some.'

Sophie rounded on him as soon as Kat had left and the three of them were leaving the hall. 'Have you no qualms about imposing yourself on other people?' She didn't know what made her angrier—his high-handed attitude or her treacherous desire to have him by her side.

'We are merely walking in the same direction,' he told her calmly when they were outside.

That was another thing that got on her nerves—that utter self-confidence which gave him the ability to persist when other men would have fallen by the wayside. Was he that certain that he would end up the victor? Or was it simply the refreshing novelty of the chase? Either way, it showed a blatant disregard for her feelings, but what could she do? It *was* a public place after all.

They walked to the market after she had deposited her boxes in her car, strolling at a pace to accommodate Jade by her side.

Sophie decided that she would not be put off her weekly enjoyment of the market just because Gregory Wallace was next to her. If he wanted to accompany her then he would jolly well discover how boring it could be to traipse around a market, waiting while she bought all her vegetables to last the week, picked out the best fruit to take home, fingered all the fabrics at the curtain stall, which she did every week and only very occasionally buying anything.

Unfortunately, he showed no signs of boredom. He examined the fruit with her, murmuring helpful little remarks, which she steadfastly ignored, until, with amusement in his voice, he said into her ear, 'You're a stubborn little minx, aren't you? Now, where did you get that from? Mother or father?'

His breath tickled her ear and she rubbed it.

'And,' he continued, 'your arms must be killing you. Why don't you relent and let me help you carry one of them? You won't be compromising your principles, you know.'

Sophie offered him a long, scathing stare and he grinned.

Arrogance she could deal with. Boorishness she could handle. Amusement was something that wore her down.

'Oh, very well,' she said finally. 'You can carry the lot. I may as well get my worth out of you being here.' She handed him all the bags and folded her arms. 'Happy now?'

'Never happier than when lugging around heavy goods,' he said, almost laughing but not quite. 'You for-get—I'm a builder.'

'I doubt you've ever lifted anything heavier than an ornament in your entire life,' she replied, moving along and allowing Jade to wander off as long as she remained within sight.

Gregory laughed, a deep-throated laugh that made her skin burn. 'In which case, I'm grateful for the practice,' he managed to get out, while next to him Sophie walked on, her head held high, ignoring the looks of interest they were generating. More gossip for other people's mental scrapbooks, she thought with resignation.

Out of habit she stopped at the curtain stall and gazed at the bolts of fabric. It was always her intention to make something. Cushions, curtains, something. The cloth always looked so tempting.

'Don't tell me that you're an expert seamstress as well,' Gregory said next to her, and after an hour of his company she couldn't summon up the energy to be annoyed.

'Not at the moment,' she replied absent-mindedly, 'although I keep intending to put it on my agenda. Now that Jade's started school full time I have quite a bit more time on my hands. Unfortunately,' she felt compelled to add, 'I'm not very good when it comes to doing fiddly things with cloth.'

'Hence the invention of the sewing machine!'

'Well, they have yet to invent one for the likes of me.' It seemed to be happening again—that sneaking feeling of contentment which occasionally reared its head when she was with him. One minute she would be foul-tempered and the next totally at ease, as though talking to him was the most natural thing in the world.

'Jade seems to love it here,' he said thoughtfully. 'That must be one of the great advantages of bringing children up in the country. A lot more freedom.'

'Yes,' Sophie said bluntly. 'I never once regretted my decision to come back here to live after I had Jade.' Now, why, she wondered, had she said *that*?

'Has your ex-husband ever been back to…visit?' Gregory wasn't looking at her when he asked this, neither was she looking at him. Perhaps that was why, she thought, it was so much easier to chat.

'Never. Not once. He's well ensconced abroad. He sends Jade a birthday present and a Christmas present. I guess in due course she'll become curious about him. Perhaps vice versa.' She shrugged. That thought had crossed her mind more than once, and she had always shoved it away because she had no idea what she would do should such a situation ever arise.

'And what,' he asked, pursuing the conversation and reaching into her head to extract her worry, 'would you do if that happened?'

'I don't know.' She stopped walking and looked at Jade, who was paying great attention to what an elderly couple was saying to her. 'I suppose I shall cross that bridge when I get to it.' Another bridge. Life sometimes seemed full of them.

'Do you want to have dinner with me tonight?' His voice was flat, without inflection, and she knew that he wouldn't pursue the invitation if she refused. She suspected, in fact, that he would stop pursuing her altogether if she refused.

Wasn't that what she'd wanted from the very beginning? The minute she'd first laid eyes on him back in the library—a lifetime ago, it seemed—he'd sent a jolt through her. It was as though she'd been sleepwalking, and suddenly, along he'd come and snapped his fingers, forcing her out of her reverie. And she'd hated it. Hadn't she?

Until his appearance in her life she'd never considered how carefully she had been tending her solitude, like a fragile orchid to be maintained in all conditions. Of course, she bustled about, talking, chatting to other people, but with the reserve of someone who remains a stranger in their midst.

His presence forced her to question the path she had chosen. She knew now that if she said no he would shrug and leave her to get on with her life.

'There are no good restaurants in this area,' she said eventually, her reserve holding her back from responding in an outright positive manner but unable to refuse because, in a confused way, she didn't want to imagine returning to her sleepwalking state.

She also knew that what he saw in her was the attraction of a challenge. Where Alan had seen beauty, naïvete and a certain—he used to tell her in the beginning—beguiling ingenuousness, Gregory saw the mature adult—cool, detached, wary, suspicious. She would be, she knew, a diversion, someone to be enjoyed until conquered. She accepted that with her usual pragmatic logic and wasn't repelled by it. Her experience with Alan had immunised her against foolish romanticism.

Maybe, she acknowledged, the time had come for her to re-enter the big, wide world—time to admit that her self-enforced emotional isolation needed to come to an end.

With Gregory she would never fear emotional involvement. He wanted that as little as she did. Whatever man she eventually found, if any, would be above all else *ordinary*.

'We could go to London,' he suggested, 'if a baby-sitter for Jade could be arranged at this late notice...'

They strolled along, neither looking at the other, as they discussed this. Jade ambled up to them, looked up, smiled and then gestured to indicate that she was hungry.

'Perhaps,' Sophie said, grasping her daughter's hand and heading in the direction of the car, 'you could call me a bit later. I can see what I can do about babysitting arrangements.'

That, as it turned out, was as easy as she'd known it would be. Kat offered to babysit. Kat, she thought wryly, would have done pretty much anything, so enormous was her stupefaction that Sophie was actually going to agree to a dinner date with Gregory, without a carrot dangling at the end of the invitation.

'You will fill me in on *everything*—,' Kat ordered that evening after she had come around in her best, as she put, painting and colouring outfit.

Sophie, who had taken extraordinary care with her choice of clothes, grinned at her friend's reflection in the hall mirror. 'There won't be anything to fill you in *on*,' she said, peering at her reflection. She had chosen to wear black—good, old, reliable black, but short for once and enlivened by strands of costume jewellery around her neck. Her hair she had left loose and it fell in jumbled coils around her shoulders and down her back. Against the sombre colour of her dress it gleamed like fire, a thing with life of its own.

'You were right though,' she said seriously, turning to face Kat, 'I need to get out a bit more. I can't bury myself here and pretend that time is at a standstill. I won't allow Alan to leave me that legacy.'

'I always told you that I knew best,' Kat said comfortably. 'But will there be romance, I wonder?'

'I'm too jaded for romance.' Sophie laughed, absolutely convinced of that one thing if nothing else. 'And Gregory is too worldly wise for it.'

'Ah...glad you established that little fact.' Spoiling the gravity of her voice, she winked, and they carried on chatting in the kitchen until, half an hour later, Gregory arrived.

The drive to London which in her car would have taken for ever passed by silently and quickly in his.

It had been some time since she had re-visited her old stamping ground, but she felt no nostalgia for the place. It was crowded—unpleasantly so after the remoteness of Ashdown.

'Do you miss it at all?' Gregory asked, as he manoeuvred down the streets towards Knightsbridge.

'Not in the slightest.'

'Because your memories of it are unwelcome or because it's London?'

If she was ever going to become part of society once more Sophie knew that she would have to open up a little. She knew that she would have to stop acting as though casually interested questions were a threat to her well-being.

'A bit of both,' she answered, uncomfortable with this brand of honesty, to which she was so ill accustomed.

'You must have enjoyed it once,' he said, slowing as they neared the restaurant. There would be no problem with parking. His driver was waiting for them, ready to take the car and return with it later.

'Once.' That was as far as she could go and he seemed to sense this because he tactfully changed the subject. A minute or two later they were out of the car, a few seconds, no more, in the bracing winter air, then they were inside the restaurant, which was warm and plush and with enough talk and laughter to save it from being too formal. It was a lively, busy place but with the advantages of intimate lighting and tables that weren't claustrophobically close.

The Italian owner greeted Gregory like an old friend and showed them to one of the more private tables towards the back, then produced two flamboyant menus with a flourish.

'I'm more than a little surprised that you accepted my invitation,' Gregory told her, when they were halfway through their starters and polite forays into conversation had eased some of her tension.

'Yes.' She finished the last of her prawns and made a few appreciative noises. Delicious. As most non-calorie-controlled food tended to be. The white wine was also quite delicious, and she sipped a few mouthfuls, allowing it to relax her.

'As ever, I just can't seem to stop you from holding forth, can I?' But it was said with lazy amusement as he looked at her across the table. 'Have you always been this talkative?'

Sophie blushed and a glimmer of a shy smile crossed her face. As always, he had no hesitation in exploring.

Was it a game for him—these attempts to prise her out of herself? And in the end did it matter?

'Believe it or not, there was a time when I was quite…normal,' she said awkwardly. She fiddled with the stem of her wine glass, paused while the wine waiter refilled it, then took a long mouthful.

'Normal?' He laughed. 'You make it sound as though you've grown fangs and taken to sleeping in coffins at night.'

That made her laugh as well, a genuine, spontaneous laugh that took her by surprise. 'Oh, dear, you've discovered my secret.' She looked at him and grinned. When she should have looked away she found she couldn't. He held her stare for so long that she felt as though her breath had caught in her throat.

The arrival of the main course, on gigantic white plates, broke the moment, but as they ate and chatted she could feel the nervous edge inside her. There was a fleeting moment when she wondered, worriedly, whether she had done the right thing.

It was all right to decide to come out of her hiding place, and it made sense that if she were to be led by the hand then it might just as well be the hand of someone to whom she was attracted, safe in the knowledge that attraction didn't last and as such could never seriously threaten her. But she would never allow herself to be hurt again, and deep inside her something was telling her that this man could hurt her.

She disregarded the mental warning. She had spent years constructing her defences and they would stand her in good stead. To be on the safe side, she began to chat about Ashdown and the endearing peculiarities of all the people who lived there, many of whom she had known since childhood.

'Different, now, of course since—'

'My housing estate,' he finished dryly for her, and she shot him a well-I-didn't-say-it look from under her lashes.

'It had to happen,' she said philosophically. 'Everywhere's being developed at a rate. To be honest, I'm surprised that Ashdown has remained untouched for such a long time.'

'Sometimes it's good for places to be developed to some extent,' he mused as their plates were cleared away and dessert declined. 'Brings in new jobs, encourages enterprise. Stops them from stagnation.'

'I shall view construction sites in a completely different light now,' Sophie said with a grin, enjoying his conversation. She decided that it was already doing her good to be out of Ashdown for a change and in the company of someone who wasn't an utterly familiar face. The wine made her feel warm and responsive.

'And what about builders?' he asked softly. 'Any chance that you might view *them* in a new light as well?'

There was a brief moment of absolute silence, then she looked him straight in the eye.

'I'll be perfectly honest with you, Gregory...I'm not looking for any kind of relationship. That may sound cold and callous, but the fact is that I've recently found myself thinking...thinking that I ought to get out a bit more. Kat's been nagging me for ages, telling me that I was wasting my life away, but I never saw it like that.'

She took a deep breath and plunged on. 'As I'm sure you may have deduced by now—' phrasing it in such a formal way seemed to take the sting out of it '—my last relationship with a man was an utter disaster. My marriage collapsed as I found myself about to have a baby, and the two things, coming all at once...' She shrugged, finding it easier to relate this than she would have expected. It helped, she supposed, that she wasn't telling him anything that he didn't already know. 'I shut myself away, I won't deny it, but I do need to get out a bit more and—'

'As such you can find it in yourself to use me for this purpose?'

Was he upset by this? Annoyed? Insulted? She couldn't tell because his voice remained bland and emotionless.

'That's a cynical way of putting it…'

'Tell me something—if I hadn't come along when I did, would anyone else have done the job?'

'You're insulted. I'm sorry…' Sophie faltered, understanding why he was offended by what she had said and realising that she had sounded worse than cold and callous. She hadn't meant to—she just hadn't explained things properly. Her desire to be honest had turned her words into weapons.

'Never mind my feelings. Just answer my question. Would anyone else have done in the situation?'

'It's not as it sounds,' she said, with some of her old fire. 'I didn't wake up one day and decide that the time had come to get out, and there you were—an available passport for the purpose.'

'No? Then why don't you try explaining?'

'This is useless. I shouldn't have said anything.' She stood up and he signalled for the bill. While he paid she excused herself and went to the cloakroom, where she found, to her consternation, that sheer misery was stamped all over her face. Her eyes were over-bright, she was on the verge of tears and she looked very pale.

She took a few deep breaths and went back out. She played her composed part as the owner emerged from the bowels of the restaurant to shake Gregory's hand warmly, waving aside modestly their joint compliments on the quality of the food.

The driver, ever efficient, was waiting for them, and as they slid into the back seat Gregory turned to face her.

'Where to?'

'Where to?' She looked at him with some amazement. She was surprised that he hadn't hailed the nearest taxi to take her back to Ashdown.

'My apartment's just round the corner.'

'*Your apartment?*' She was beginning to sound like a parrot, and she cleared her throat, before continuing. 'I thought...'

'That I was twisted with rage at what you said?' He leaned forward and told his driver to take him to his apartment. Then he relaxed and surveyed her coolly. 'I am merely curious to find out how you intended to finish what you began to say.'

'I thought I *had* finished.' She pulled her coat closer around her and kept her body perfectly still.

'I don't think so,' he drawled, 'which is why I think this conversation needs to be continued somewhere more private. Why don't you telephone Kat and tell her that you might be back a little later than you originally thought?' He reached into his inside pocket and handed her his mobile phone.

Sophie looked at it for some while, then took it from him. What was going on? It was time to find out.

CHAPTER EIGHT

CONVERSATION in the car was limited and stilted. Sophie's occasional comments were met with clipped answers, and for most part Gregory remained broodingly silent in the semi-darkness of the back seat.

That suited her. Her brief stab at total honesty had met with such cold disdain that she had been prepared to retreat swiftly and comprehensively back into her fortress. To find herself now *en route* to his apartment threw her into a state of complete confusion.

Fortunately, his place was close, and before she could launch into another abortive attempt at small talk the driver had pulled up outside an impressive crescent of Victorian houses, cream-painted with black wrought-iron railings at the front and three steps up to the front doors. Understated, but reeking of well-bred good taste.

Gregory leaned forward to issue a few instructions to his driver, then led the way to his house. A house it was, but once inside Sophie realised that there was much more of a bachelor apartment feel to it—the sort of subdued, unobtrusively elegant place which would have had her ex-husband watering at the mouth.

There was almost no clutter, and the spaciousness was emphasised by wooden flooring which gave it a light, airy feel. The paintings on the walls were mostly abstract or cubist, and through open doors she could make out scattered rugs and warm, vibrant colours.

He led her straight through to a small, comfortable sitting room just beyond the downstairs cloakroom, and gestured to her to have a seat.

Interview time, she thought, trying not to feel cowed. In a minute he'll rattle off a series of questions, I shall struggle with the answers, fail the test and be sent home on the next train from Paddington.

'I'll have something non-alcoholic,' she said, when she saw him pour himself a whisky and soda and then turn to her, his eyebrows raised questioningly.

He handed her a glass of mineral water, which she nervously accepted, watching him warily as he lowered himself onto the two-seater sofa next to her. Couldn't he have chosen another chair? There were three perfectly acceptable ones in the room and all of them would have put more distance between them.

'So,' he began, 'you were saying...?' It was as though the interruption to their conversation in the restaurant had been a matter of a few seconds.

Sophie crossed her legs and leaned forward nervously, with the glass resting between her hands on her knee. 'I was saying...' she started, unable to look him in the face and concentrating on the bay window behind his shoulder. 'Oh, what's the point?' She drank a few mouthfuls of water, one hand cradling her elbow.

'The point is,' Gregory said in a cool, controlled voice, 'I'm interested to hear where your arguments were going.'

'Why?'

'Because...' he swallowed a mouthful of whisky and soda, taking his time with the conversation '...aside from anything else, I've never heard a woman put forward a reason for embarking on a relationship from a purely business point of view.'

'But you've heard a few men do it?' She glanced at him cynically. 'I've been through enough to know that romance is an illusion, and throwing yourself into a relationship is just downright stupid.'

'That's quite a sweeping statement.'

'Is it?' Sophie looked at him narrowly. 'I think it's just common sense to try and avoid mistakes that you've made in the past. Aren't we supposed to learn from our experiences?'

'Learn, yes. But there are degrees of learning.'

'You didn't know my ex-husband,' she muttered under her breath.

'So,' he said softly, clinically, 'you're proposing…what?' He deposited his drink on the table in front of them and proceeded to give her a long, speculative stare.

Now that she had uttered what had been in her mind, now that she had stated her interest in having some sort of relationship with him—however far removed from love that relationship might be—she could feel herself getting cold feet. It was one thing to contemplate a certain course of action but quite another when the practicalities of any such course of action were brought out into the open and discussed.

She also didn't like the picture of herself as someone cold and calculating, willing to use someone else, because that simply wasn't how she thought of herself, but she knew that her words told a different story.

'I'm not proposing anything,' she said, finishing her drink with some reluctance because she no longer had anything to do with her hands. 'I shouldn't have mentioned…anything at all. I apologise.'

'And I'm supposed to let it go at that?'

'That's right.'

It was clear from his tone of voice that he had no intention of letting anything go, and she could understand why. It was like being given all the elements of a riveting piece of gossip, all the elements but the crucial one that makes sense of the rest.

'Why did you decide on me?' he asked curiously, and she looked at him frankly.

'Because you're an attractive man,' she said, without hesitation, 'and because…' this was trickier to explain '…I know that I would never have to be worried about…falling for you.'

'How flattering.'

'It's not meant to be an insult,' Sophie said, frowning. 'I'm sure that there are thousands of women who would fall for you at the drop of a hat. But not me, and that's…that's almost part of your attraction,' she confessed. 'I feel safe…' Her voice petered out because she couldn't quite find the right words to express what she had to say.

'You wouldn't risk putting yourself in the position of being hurt again?'

'Yes, I suppose that's it. Yes, that's it.' Her fingers fidgeted nervously. Was she having this conversation? It depressed her to think that she had reached a stage where she was prepared to sleep with a man simply because she harboured no fears of being hurt by him. Gregory Wallace could walk out on her, she knew, and she would be able to carry on because she was well defended against men such as him.

Well, she thought mutinously, what's wrong with that? There were thousands of women the world over—millions—who slept with men for no other reason that they were physically attracted to them, and she could freely admit that she was attracted to Gregory. Her body responded to him in a way that left her breathless, and she had given up trying to pretend otherwise.

'Of course,' she felt compelled to add, 'as human beings go, you're perfectly passable.'

The features of his face lightened for an instant and

he laughed out loud. 'As human beings go, I'm perfectly passable? What does that mean in lay person's terms?'

Sophie blushed and tilted her chin defensively. 'I mean…that you can be quite…good company.' That was as far as she was prepared to go on the subject.

'So you…quite…like me. Is that it?'

'I suppose so, yes. Except for those times, of course, when I can't stand you.' That made perfect sense to her, although she didn't care for the look of gravity on his face when she said that. Was he laughing at her? She tried to second-guess what was going through his mind and failed.

'Don't you feel just a little nostalgic for the romantic person you must have been a few years ago?' He retrieved his glass from the table, took a sip of what was now virtually all water, winced and then rose to get himself another drink. He offered her one in passing, which she accepted with alacrity.

This was turning out to be far more difficult than she had anticipated. A stiff something or other might dispel some of the nervous tension raging inside her.

She hoped, as he handed her a drink a minute later, that he had forgotten his question, but she could tell from the quizzical look on his face that he was waiting for her answer, and she shrugged dismissively. These were the sorts of questions that she hated most of all, the ones that needled their way under her skin and extracted the young, starry-eyed girl she had once been.

'A little.' She looked down into her glass and shrugged again. 'Sometimes.' He didn't rush in with patronising words of advice, which would instantly have had her back up, and she found herself saying, with rather more emotion than she intended, 'Sometimes I wish that I could just go back in time. Redo things, act with the benefit of hindsight. But then, when I find myself thinking like that, I remember that were it not for Alan I wouldn't have Jade—and Jade has been my greatest of joys. Mostly I just accept that the past is something I have to release so that it can release me in turn. Does that make any sense?' She raised her eyes to his, and in the shadowy darkness of the room felt her heartbeat quicken.

'So.' She gave a brittle laugh, breaking the atmosphere between them quite deliberately because for a second there it had totally destabilised her for reasons she couldn't quite put her finger on. 'What you see before you is someone utterly immune to romance, hence my utterly unromantic proposition. All I can do is apologise if I offended you. I'm more than happy to pretend that this conversation never happened. In fact,' she continued too brightly, 'I really must telephone Kat and let her know that we're on our way.'

She rested her glass on the table and was about to stand up when Gregory said, without moving and in a low, even voice, 'Tell her to expect you in the morning.'

'What?'

He handed her his mobile phone for the second time that evening, and she gave it a long, searching look, as though trying to extract a few answers from it.

'You've opened a door, Sophie. there's no point trying to close it again.'

'Are you saying…? *What* are you saying?' Her heart was racing and her mouth was dry with a mixture of apprehension and, if she were to be honest with herself, excitement.

'I'm no romantic fool myself,' he told her, fixing her with his eyes, not allowing her to look away from his face. 'I may not have been through an appalling marriage, like you, but I've seen enough to know that you're right. Romance is for teenagers whose heads are stuffed full of dreams. It has very little place in reality.'

She nodded in understanding but felt, all the same, a perplexing stab of disappointment.

'I find you intriguing, Sophie,' he said huskily, 'but, then, I suppose you've already worked that out for yourself.'

Yes, she *had* worked that out for herself, but to hear him say it now, here, in the intimacy of these surroundings, made her body tremble lightly. She took the phone from him, and found that her hands were shaking as she dialled her home number. It rang three times before Kat answered, and she assumed as light a voice as possible as she explained that she would be unable to get back this evening.

'Rather a lot to drink, Kat,' she said, in a way which was meant to sound vague but somehow emerged sounding mysterious. She added a few pleasantries as she tried to douse the curiosity bursting down the line, then she pressed the button to end the call and handed the phone back to Gregory.

This is crazy, Sophie's mind was telling her over and over again. Crazy, crazy, crazy. What happens now? How on earth could she have ever entertained this idea? Maybe she had been going through some kind of mental instability, a period of premature middle-aged crisis. For heaven's sake, if she had had to emerge from her cocoon, why pick this man of all men?

If she had contemplated a future with a man as involving someone kind, thoughtful and maybe a little dull, why not just wait until she met him? Why allow insanity to drag her down this road? Her only excuse was that he wouldn't be able to hurt her!

She was frowning, contemplating all these things in fleeting thoughts which were like flashes of quicksilver, when he leant over very slowly and cupped her nape with his hand.

Immediately she froze, but then, almost as quickly, she turned to fire as his mouth met hers in a long, searching kiss. They were leaning towards one another and she placed her hands flat against his chest, tilting her head as his lips explored her mouth, a lingering exploration that sent all her thoughts—wild and practical, hesitant and certain—flying in every direction.

This was why she had started this whole thing. Without trying to find the sensible answer, instinct had pointed her in the right way. The attraction she acknowledged that she felt for him was far more powerful than her head had given it credit for, and her body, needing the fulfilment she knew he could give, had sought it out but under cover of reason. She'd lived for so long with her head guiding her emotions that even when she'd acknowledged her growing attraction to him she'd still continued to conduct a one-way argument on her reaction, based on the practical, cool-headed logic that had seen her through the past few years.

She could feel the control ebbing out of her body as his lips lowered to her neck. Her breasts, pulsing against her dress, ached to be touched.

'Are you sure you want to go through with this?' he whispered, and she nodded.

'I think I've wanted to go through with this for longer than I care to admit,' she said honestly, and she could tell from his groan as he buried his face against her neck that the thought of that fired a response in him.

'Why on earth didn't you say something sooner? Why the avoidance games?'

'They weren't avoidance games,' Sophie murmured, breathing quickly and clasping her fingers in his hair. 'I really wasn't looking for any kind of…affair…with anyone. It just took me by surprise.'

To feel his dark hair slip against her fingers was wonderful. It had been such a long time since she had felt anything for a man that the sensation was as powerful as if she were a virgin, dipping her toes into her own sexuality for the very first time.

'My bedroom is upstairs.' His voice was low and unsteady, and for a moment they drew away from one another. When she looked into his eyes she seemed to be reading what was there for the first time. He wanted her to consider what lay ahead of her. She had talked to him logically and coolly and had revealed, as much as she seemed able, what lay in her heart—her need to involve herself with him, which had fought a battle against her desire to ignore the temptation.

Now, as they stared at one another, she knew that he was giving her a chance. A chance to walk away.

Walking away was something she couldn't do.

'Yes,' she said in a clear, low voice.

They held hands as they mounted the stairs. Very adolescent, she thought, but she liked her fingers linked through his. It felt natural. As they reached the top of the staircase he rubbed his thumb against her skin and a shiver of pleasure ran through her.

His bedroom was at the far end of the landing. It was high-ceilinged, like the rest of the house she had glimpsed, with the same masculine sparseness about it. She saw all this first in darkness, with her eyes acclimatising to the shapes in the room, then more clearly as he switched on a small lamp on the dressing-table and the room was filled with a dull glow.

He turned to face her, not saying anything, and slowly began to remove his clothes.

The thought of backing away now never even entered

her mind. When she moved to begin undressing he stilled her with his hand and smiled so she remained where she was and looked at him instead—a frank, open appraisal of his body, its long, supple lines, its implicit strength.

'I take back what I said,' she told him, when he was fully unclothed aside from his boxer shorts.

'You've changed your mind?' Underneath the casualness of his voice she could discern a sudden tension that made her pulses race.

'Yes.' Sophie grinned at him. 'About you never having lifted anything heavier than an ornament.' She reached out and trailed one finger along his shoulder blades, then down the centre of his torso, ending at the waistband of his boxers.

He caught her hand and pulled her towards him.

'You witch,' he said, with a laugh in his voice. His hands found the zip of her dress and he pulled it down, then eased it off her shoulders, taking his time.

After Alan, Sophie had thought that she could never let a man near her body again. The thought of it had filled her with revulsion. She knew that over time she had given off signals, indicated with body language that she was not open to advances. Now, as Gregory's hands smoothed down her back, she was finding it difficult to hold back. Her body felt as though it had been starved.

The dress slipped to the floor and lay around her ankles, and was followed by her bra, which was a blessed relief. Now she felt as though she could breathe a little more easily.

'You're beautiful,' Gregory said unevenly.

'I'm tempted to return the compliment,' Sophie whispered back, 'but it might go to your head.' They walked towards the bed, and she could feel her heart pounding against her ribcage. As she settled on the mattress she sighed and closed her eyes.

His hands moved slowly over her, over every inch of her body, pulling down her underwear and brushing against her thighs. It was an unhurried exploration, almost as if he were trying to commit her body to memory.

She turned onto her side and ran her hands along his body, delighting in the feel of him, and their leisurely touches assumed a more urgent tone.

When he bent to caress her breasts with his mouth the sensation was so powerfully erotic that she felt as if she might explode. She arched slightly, raising her nipples to his mouth, and moaned, gasping, as his tongue played with the throbbing peaks. His hand travelled the length of her body, parted her legs and began to rouse her intimately so that her panting grew quicker and she squirmed against his fingers.

She half opened her eyes as his head inched its way down her body, and when he removed his fingers from her she felt the cool moistness of his tongue replace them. This was the first time that she had ever been caressed in this way and the pleasure was exquisite. Alan, underneath the suave, charming exterior, had never enjoyed making love and that was something which had always transmitted itself to her whenever he'd touched her. Gregory, she was quickly realising, was a true sensualist and her body responded accordingly.

Their movements were now becoming hungrier, more urgent. When he straightened to kiss her she reached down and felt him stiff in her hands, but he couldn't let her caress him—he was too close to the edge.

'What about contraception?' he asked, and she realised with a start that that was something to which she had paid little heed.

'I'm in a safe period,' she said, relieved as she rapidly worked out her dates in her head.

He kissed her again, more slowly this time, and as he eased himself into her she had the most amazing feeling of doing the right thing. She must have been starved, she thought dazedly, of physical closeness. More so than she had ever dreamt possible. He moved against her and together they built up a steadily increasing rhythm until neither could hold on any longer. The release was a long, shuddering, overwhelming escape from the body. It seemed to last for ever. How was that possible? It was glorious.

When he finally lay next to her she flipped onto her stomach and looked at him.

'Well?' he said lazily, stroking her hair away from her face. 'Do we have an examination now on the act of love-making, you strange little creature?'

'Hardly little.' She laughed throatily, enjoying his nearness, having fought it for such a long time.

'And if I ask you whether the earth moved for you, would you lie and tell me that it did?'

'Oh, please!' Sophie exclaimed in a shocked voice, propping herself on her elbows to scrutinise his face. 'Surely you don't need cheap boosts for your ego!'

He looked at her and gave her a crooked smile, which made it very difficult to think that this was a man who was probably worth millions.

'OK. The earth moved!' She grinned at him, pleasurably content, then she sighed. 'I have to tell you…' It occurred to her at this point that she really didn't have to tell him anything if she didn't want to, but for some reason she found that she did. 'Alan was…not a very considerate lover. Of course, naïve as I was, I didn't know differently.'

'Meaning that you were a virgin when you met him?'

'Are you shocked?'

'I'm…several things, but shocked isn't one of them.' He wasn't smiling when he said this, and for a second she was tempted to ask him to clarify but she didn't.

She rolled onto her back and stared up at the ceiling, traveling back in time and viewing the past through the cold eyes of maturity. 'I never imagined that love-making could be as…satisfying as it just was.' She could feel herself getting tearful at the thought of all that lost innocence and stifled it. 'I suppose that's going to send that oversized ego of yours soaring through the roof, but there you have it.'

'It's very honest of you to tell me,' Gregory said, pulling her towards him so that they were now both on their sides, facing one another.

He casually ran his finger along her breasts, circling one nipple, which she felt harden at his touch. *How could he do that?* They had only just finished making love and here she was, her body stirring into life once again when she should be sated and ready for a long sleep. She took a deep, steadying breath and said as flippantly as she could manage. 'Well, I'm a very honest person.'

'So I've noticed.'

'I was a fool to have ever married the man,' she said bitterly, admitting it for the first time aloud. 'An utter idiot. Thank heavens for Jade and thank heavens for the fact that at least I've learnt a thing or two from the experience.'

Gregory didn't say anything, but for a split second his hand faltered in its meanderings. 'I can't remember ever asking a woman this before,' he said eventually, 'but what happens next?'

Sophie laughed a little at that. 'You've *never* asked a woman that before?'

'I've never had to.'

She gave him a long, critical look, which finally he returned with a protesting one of his own, then she said, 'Well, I should rather like to carry on with…this…but if you think not then that's not a problem.'

'You'd just get up, get dressed and walk away.' His voice had hardened slightly and she shrugged.

'I might get a taxi. Ashdown's a little far for walking.' She had meant that as a joke, to break the sudden coolness she felt radiating from him, but in the event he just continued to stare at her, his eyes glittering in the dim shadows of the bedroom.

'Look,' Sophie said, abandoning the attempt at humour and feeling obliged to repeat what she had said to him before, 'I'm attracted to you but I'm not going to let you, or anyone else for that matter, hurt me. I like you because I know your measure.'

She could tell that what she was saying wasn't going down all that well, and rather than plunge onwards and in the process end up saying all the wrong things—or at least all the right things but worded in the wrong way—she inhaled deeply, counted to ten and then continued, 'I thought we'd been through all this.'

'You're right,' he said abruptly, 'we have. There's nothing more to be said on the subject.

Sophie looked at him dubiously, and she could sense the effort as he altered his tone back to one of light, amused acceptance of the situation. 'But what about all those gossips…? They'll have a field day, you know, if we see each other in public.'

'Won't they?' Sophie's eyes gleamed at the thought of that. 'They're all such dears, really. We'll almost be doing them a favour, by giving them lots of talk about.'

'Mmm.' Gregory rubbed his chin thoughtfully, then cupped her heavy breast in his hand. 'In other words,

148   A RELUCTANT WIFE

we could almost be said to be doing a spot of charity work by consorting with one another.'

'Absolutely.'

'In that case, shall we spend a bit more time, preparing ourselves for this spot of charity work?' He got to his feet and switched off the lamp, throwing the room into darkness so that when they made love this time it was even more thrillingly erotic, if that were possible.

Well, she thought the following morning as they drove back to Ashdown, Kat *had* said a million times that she needed to get back to the land of the living. She stole a sideways glance at Gregory and decided that she had certainly returned to the land of the living with gusto. It had been a happy choice. She couldn't remember when she had felt so alive.

And on her terms. No involvement, no agonising, no thoughts of betrayal and suffering. A relationship she could handle, and one that she knew he could as well. His objective wasn't to get married and settle down, and now, when she thought about it, she couldn't believe that she had wasted time, wondering whether she was doing the right thing.

Could it be better? What if she *had* resolved to save herself and her precarious tiptoeing into the outside world for when the right man came along? How cautious she would have been, and she wouldn't have been exempt from worrying about whether Mr Right would let her down. She exhaled a sigh of rare happiness and settled back in her seat to doze. She didn't know what time they'd finally got to sleep that night, but it had been very late.

She awoke when the car was slowing and pulling into the short drive to her house.

'Well timed, Sleeping Beauty,' Gregory said with lazy amusement.

'Yes,' Sophie agreed with a dry grin, 'you timed that drive very well to accommodate my nap.'

'Shall I come in with you?'

Sophie thought that she would have liked nothing better, but she shook her head slowly. 'No. I need to have a word with Kat and Jade might become a little confused if she sees us entering together.' She looked at him evenly. 'Why don't you give me a call and we can arrange to meet up…?'

'Right.' He leaned his head back against the windowpane and looked at her with such sexual intimacy that she could feel her cheeks redden. It never failed to startle her how a single glance from him could reduce her to girlishness, and she assumed that she had become so unaccustomed to a man in her life that she had forgotten the impact one had.

Kat was waiting when she entered the house, her eyes glowing with unasked questions. While she spent some time with her daughter she could see Kat hovering, virtually hopping from foot to foot, ready to explode.

She settled Jade in front of her homework, and Kat immediately rounded on her, barely able to get her questions out in logical order.

'Yes. We're an item,' Sophie said at last, when the series of questions had fizzled out into expectant silence.

'You're an item? What does *that* mean?'

'It means that…we're going out with one another.' Sophie strolled towards the kettle, made them both a cup of coffee and remained where she was, leaning against the kitchen counter. The news appeared to have rendered her friend momentarily speechless.

'I thought you didn't like "the man", as you were fond of calling him.'

'I guess I was wrong.'

Kat remained silent for a while, then she said thoughtfully, 'You'll be careful, won't you, Soph?'

'What on earth do you mean?'

'Gregory Wallace looks as though he has the potential to break hearts.'

Sophie laughed. 'Oh, no. Not mine, Kat! You forget I've been down that road before. I know how to steer well clear of the landmarks! No…we understand each other. He's not looking for commitment and neither am I.' She held the mug between her hands and carefully took a few sips, blowing on it in between. 'I know him for what he is and I can enjoy being with him because I know the limits around him. Do you understand what I'm saying?'

Kat looked at her worriedly. 'I know what you're *trying* to say, Soph, but life isn't as…as *controllable* as you think it is. I mean people, situations…things happen…'

'You sound like a demented fortune-teller! Look,' Sophie said reassuringly, 'I'm not the gullible little girl I was years ago. I've spent years building up a shell, protecting myself… I'll be absolutely fine. At least I know that however witty and charming and good-looking and knowledgeable Gregory Wallace is he's still Mr Wrong. Now, I'd be worried if I had launched my grand debut with someone a little less elevated, someone I might find myself…well, you know what I'm saying…'

She drank some coffee and frowned. What was the third degree all about anyway? she thought irritably. Why was it that Kat couldn't see things the way *she* could? It all seemed so obvious to her, but translating it into words was more difficult than she had expected.

She promptly changed the subject, but underneath the cheerful banter she knew that her friend was still anxious. Sophie was at a loss how to tell Kat that nothing would happen, that it was a purely physical thing. How on earth, Sophie thought, could Kat fail to understand that? It was hardly as though Kat belonged to the school of women who rigorously saved themselves for Mr Right.

It just wasn't a problem.

She kept repeating the refrain to herself over the next six weeks as her attraction to Gregory, if anything, became stronger.

She did her utmost to keep Jade out of the scenario, not wanting her to be hurt when she and Gregory parted company sooner or later, but after a while she found herself growing lazy simply because Jade and Gregory seemed to get along so well.

She had no idea how long she could have continued with her pleasurable lifestyle but Fate, working conscientiously behind the scenes, appeared in all her glory and turned Sophie's world upside down.

CHAPTER NINE

THE thought had been niggling away at the back of Sophie's mind for a couple of days, but as she dropped off Jade at school and headed towards the library it became less of a niggle and more of a tidal wave.

She had missed a period.

They'd been very careful every single time they'd made love. They'd used protection, and Sophie had even debated whether she should do something rather more satisfactory about the situation and visit her local family planning clinic.

But still. Her period was two weeks late and there *had* been that one night, that first time.

Once the thought took root it grew with frightening speed, and by the time midday rolled around she found that she could hardly think clearly. At precisely twelve-thirty she told Claire that she had to go to the supermarket, the large one half an hour's drive away, and that she might not be back until after two. Claire accepted it with her usual equanimity.

The drive there seemed to take for ever, but perversely Sophie hadn't wanted to go to the local chemist's. She couldn't imagine handing over that little box to Mrs Drayton at the counter. The whispers surrounding her and Gregory, after their initial flurry, had died down as people accepted seeing them together. She had no intention of rekindling them with the purchase of a pregnancy testing kit.

She was rekindling them needlessly, she told herself

as she drove around the car park, hunting down a free space. Because she was *not pregnant*.

She found that she couldn't wait until she got back home to get the result and conveniently there was a ladies' cloakroom at the supermarket. She told herself that she needed to put her mind at peace or else she would simply spend the remainder of the afternoon in a complete dither.

The result, the little blue line appearing strongly in the box which should have remained clear, was such a resounding shock that Sophie had to lean against the cloakroom door to prevent herself from keeling over.

She stared at the little piece of plastic in her hand, and the bright blue line stared back at her until finally she made her way back to her car.

Now what? She tried to think but her body was shaking. Even her brain felt as if it was shaking. She simply couldn't think.

She was pregnant. There was no point in trying to kid herself that the result was wrong. She was carrying Gregory Wallace's child. It was the worst of all possible scenarios.

Of course, she would have to end the relationship.

She was halfway back to the village when that thought occurred to her, and the impact was such that she had to pull over into a layby to try and gather herself together.

No more Gregory Wallace, no more Mr Wrong who had somehow made life seem so suddenly right. Now, as she contemplated a future without him in it, she understood why. She had fallen in love with him. She rested her head against the steering-wheel and closed her eyes.

When had that happened? she thought with sick desperation. Before she had slept with him. For the first time she contemplated her actions in a series of flashbacks, and realised that she had slept with him for a reason—because it had seemed to be the natural thing to do, because it had made sense, because she loved him.

How on earth, she thought, could she *ever* have thought that it had only been to do with sex? How could she have been so utterly stupid? It had never crossed her mind to wonder why she had suddenly decided that the time had been right for her to emerge from her cocoon. She could hardly believe how foolish she had been, living in her blissful ignorance, working everything out so rationally in her head, confident that past experience would protect her, keep her intact.

She took a deep, shaky breath and drove back to the library, where she maintained a cheerful façade. She collected Jade from school, went home, did homework with her and cooked some fish fingers for tea, while inside her head only two thoughts played over and over again until she thought that she would go mad. She was pregnant and she was in love.

If Alan had become a blurry image, the fact of her pregnancy brought his image back to her with a clarity that left her breathless and despairing.

She remembered everything now. The pregnancy had been an accident. She had diligently been taking the Pill but, as luck would have it, two nights of a stomach bug had left her unprotected. When she'd discovered the consequences of her upset stomach Alan had hit the roof. She could see his dark, furious face in her mind as he'd stormed around their apartment; she could hear him as he'd tried to bully her into having an abortion. The scene was so clear in her head that it was almost as though it had happened yesterday.

His beautiful ornament had suddenly ceased to be beautiful, and he had made his thoughts on the matter painfully clear as the months progressed and her flat stomach began to swell. He had neither wanted fatherhood nor did he need any physical reminders of the fact.

Well, she wasn't going to give Gregory the chance to rant and rave at her stupidity. He hadn't wanted commitment and there was no way that she was going to force him into the situation. She didn't think that she could bear to live with the hurt of being rejected by him.

As soon as Jade had gone to sleep she telephoned him on his mobile phone, her fingers playing restlessly with the cord of the phone as she tried to keep her voice normal. He was about to go to a client dinner and she could picture him, striding about his room, getting dressed, looking in the mirror as an afterthought.

'I need to see you before Thursday,' she said, unable to rustle up any laughter when he chuckled and remarked that he could hardly bear the absence himself.

'I can cancel my meeting tomorrow,' he said, sensing her mood even though he was miles away and speaking down an indifferent telephone. 'Is it important?'

'We need to talk. I've been doing some thinking.' She had still not decided whether she would tell him yet about the pregnancy, but she couldn't see the point in keeping it a secret. Sooner or later he would find out. It was hardly as though she could hide the fact in a village as small as Ashdown.

'Thinking... About what?' There was a sudden stillness to his voice that made her heart flip over. Was he anxious? Worried? She tried not to let her mind stray down that path. Misery lay down there and there would be time enough to make her acquaintance with that emotion.

'I'll talk to you when I see you,' Sophie said. 'You must be running late.'

'I can scrap this damn client do and drive over to

Ashdown right now. I could be there in…under an hour and a half.'

'No… Thanks for the offer. It'll keep.' She needed some time to get herself together, and to see him so soon wouldn't do very much for her self-control

As soon as she had finished talking to him, and on the spur of the moment, she dialled Kat's number. She needed to talk. Where had this impulse come from? She had spent years never feeling the urge to pour out her feelings. Now she felt as though she had to get this thing off her chest or she would simply go mad.

'I'm on my way,' Kat said, as soon as she'd detected the shaky quality of Sophie's voice, and within fifteen minutes she was standing on the front doorstep with an expression of barely concealed alarm on her face.

'What on earth is the matter, Soph? It's not Jade, is it? Nothing's happened to Jade…?'

'No. Jade's fine. Come in.'

It was blessed relief to share her problem with someone else. She had bottled in so much of her grief and hurt after the end of her marriage that she could hardly believe what a release it was to spill this personal nightmare out to a compassionate ear.

'Oh, dear.' At the end of the garbled account, during which Sophie had broken down several times, Kat looked completely bowled over.

'Isn't it?' Sophie said in a wry, tearful voice. 'One minute I'm plodding merrily along, head in the clouds, the next minute I'm pregnant and hopelessly in love with the wrong man.'

'Maybe,' Kat said tentatively, 'the feeling's mutual?' She looked optimistically at her friend, then sighed as Sophie shot her a you-must-be-mad look in return. 'Well, what do you do from here? You can hardly leave Ashdown and run away,' Kat continued pragmatically.

'The most time you have on your side is what…three months? Maybe four if you dress cleverly? And then Gregory will know.'

'By then I would have had time to get myself together a bit more. I'm seeing him tomorrow, and I shall tell him that it's over—that I've had second thoughts. When he finds out about the pregnancy in due course I shall be strong enough to slam the door in his face.'

'He'll have a right to know his own child, Soph.'

'Men don't see things like that, Kat. Gregory's fun and, well, thoughtful and good company, but he's not looking for a long-term relationship. The prospect of a child will have him running for cover.' It helped to cast him in this unflattering light, and before her friend could jump to his defence Sophie hustled off to the kitchen to pour them both another cup of coffee.

'I suppose there's a chance,' she continued, entering the room and handing Kat her cup, 'that he'll feel financially obliged to help us out, but that's as far as it'll go.'

'And, of course, you'll fight him tooth and nail to avoid that,' Kat said, in a voice Sophie didn't much care for.

'If a financial donation clears his conscience, he can donate whatever he wants,' she said.

'This is a baby, Sophie. Your baby, yes, but *his* baby too. We're not talking about a financial donation to a charity. He'll want contact with the child—you know that and so do I. Look at how fond he is of Jade…'

Yes, Sophie had thought about that. From every angle there seemed to be no escape route, and she honestly didn't know what would happen. In a way, Alan had made things easy for her by dumping her and then vanishing comprehensively out of her life.

Gregory wasn't Alan, nor were her feelings for him in any way similar to those she'd had for her ex-husband. She loved Gregory as deeply and passionately as she thought she could ever love anyone. That in itself was terrifying because now, with this baby inside her, she could envisage years and years and years of Gregory being around, not for her but for his child. Years and years and years of having to see him, communicate with him, long after his short-lived physical attraction to her had died a death.

And what when he moved on? Fell in love himself? Got married? Had more children of his own with another woman? She would still have to see him and she would still have to endure the pain of knowing that his life was no longer a part of hers.

She found that she couldn't tell Kat all this, though. She could hardly believe, herself, how far she had fallen.

Later, when Kat had gone and there was only the silence of the house around her, she lay in bed and played the now familiar game of scenarios. She contemplated her situation from every angle and tried to envisage all the possible outcomes. It was hopeless.

She could remember lying in bed, just like this, with Alan next to her but turned away from her. She could remember his anger when she'd told him that she wasn't going to get rid of the baby simply to please him. All the insults he had thrown at her. She was nothing, he'd said, a nobody whom he had plucked from obscurity to stand alongside him, and he wouldn't tolerate her becoming a fat, sweating, pregnant mare, her astonishing beauty lost in the world of nappies and breast-feeding and sleepless nights.

The minute she'd told him about the pregnancy her body had begun to repulse him. He'd seen, he'd told her, how his mother had become over the years, how pregnancies had ruined her looks and turned her into a harridan who couldn't see beyond the children she had spawned.

At times like that there had been nothing Sophie could say, and eventually she'd given up the useless battle of trying to persuade him otherwise. She'd taken refuge in silence, watching from the sidelines as his business meetings became more and more frequent, his late nights later and later, accepting with bitter resignation the eventual infidelity.

But he had gone and left her to get on with her life, for which she was grateful. Gregory, she suspected, would not be quite so obliging.

She found, the following day, that her stomach was knotted with nerves as she awaited the approaching confrontation. They had arranged for him to come to her house at eight after Jade had gone to bed. Whereas formerly she would have been waiting for him with churning excitement, eager to see his face, hear his voice and listen to him as he told her what he had been doing, she found, at seven-thirty, that she was frozen with a sense of impending dread.

She fought down the temptation to run and hide when, at a quarter to eight, the doorbell rang. Instead, she took a deep breath, opened the front door and reluctantly allowed her eyes to travel from his shoes up to his face.

'What's the matter? he asked sharply.

He looked as though he had spent the night on the road. His face was drawn and his hair was rumpled, as if he had spent the journey running his fingers through it.

Sophie had already decided that if she was to end the relationship then she would have to appear as normal as she possibly could, if only to deflect questions. He wasn't a fool. She could tell from the way that he was looking at her, searching her face, that he could sense that something was horribly wrong.

'I've made something to eat,' Sophie said, ignoring his question and leading the way towards the kitchen. Staring at him was just going to make things harder.

'You haven't answered my question, Sophie,' he said from behind her, and before she could busy herself with the casserole in the oven he had put his hand on her shoulder and swung her to face him. 'That's better.' His hand moved from her shoulder to her neck, and from her neck to the side of her face, where it remained, caressing her cheek. He drew her closer to him, and cradled her face in his hands. 'I've missed you,' he said with a crooked smile, which made her heart flip over.

She forced herself to think that when he said that he meant that he missed sleeping with her. He didn't miss *her*. Not in the way that she had missed him, and always would.

'The casserole will burn if I don't take it out of the oven,' Sophie said. She wanted him to kiss her so badly that in a minute she would collapse if he didn't let her go and give her a few minutes, with her back to him, to get back her sanity.

'I like burnt casseroles. They have a much more distinctive flavour.' But he drew back and watched as she laid the casserole on the table, not looking at him but aware of him in a way that made her skin tingle.

'Now,' he said, as they sat facing one another and she dished out their food, 'you said that you had something to tell me. You might as well get it off your chest before you self-combust.'

He dug into a mouthful of food and looked at her impassively across the table.

'I've been thinking about us, Gregory...'

'Why?'

'Why...?' She gave him a startled look, then lowered her eyes and continued to eat. The food tasted like chalk but she forced herself to eat. 'Because—'

'Correct me if I'm wrong, but I was under the impression that you were actually enjoying what we had—unless, of course, I misread the situation, and you're more of a consummate actress than I gave you credit for.'

'No! Of course I'm not...and, yes, I was...'

'You *were*...?' He looked at her questioningly and she abandoned her desultory efforts to make headway with her food.

Now was the time to say what she had to say, but when she rested her eyes on his face all she felt was an overwhelming surge of emotion. Everything about him, in such a short space of time, now seemed so *familiar*. What would it be like when she no longer had the chance to indulge this need to look at him? When she looked at him and saw beyond him to his new mistress, his new wife, his new *life*?

'Just say what you have to say, Sophie!' He had finished what was on his plate, but for once he wasn't helping himself to more.

'I would, she wanted to shout at him, if only I could rediscover my vocal cords!

Instead, and in trembling silence she began to clear the table, taking her time as she stacked the dishwasher, where the plates and cutlery joined the dishes from that morning and those from the evening before. She resolutely switched it on, then asked Gregory if he wanted any coffee.

'I want you to stop beating around the bush.'

'All right then. I'm not sure that I can carry on seeing you.' There, she had said it. The world hadn't stopped turning, although it had felt like a close thing.

He didn't say anything for a very long time and
Sophie could feel his eyes on her as he leant back in the
chair and folded his arms.

'And what's suddenly brought this on?'

'Nothing's suddenly brought anything on,' Sophie answered, fiddling with her fingers. She made yet more
meaningless movements as she fetched two mugs from
the cupboard and made them both some coffee. A stiff
gin and tonic would calm her down, but stiff gin and
tonics were not a good idea when it came to clear thinking, and now that she had said what she wanted to say
she had a sneaking suspicion that she would need a clear
head.

'Will you stop shuffling about and sit down and talk
to me?' Gregory snapped, when she'd deposited his mug
in front of him and retreated to one of the counters with
a wet sponge.

'There's not much more to say.' Sophie remained
where she was, frozen in the process of wiping the
counter. 'I mean, we could go over the whole thing, but
that would just be a pointless trip through the trees.'

'I'm in the mood for pointless trips,' he said grimly.

Sophie sighed and gave a little shrug. As he sat and
stared at her, frowning darkly, he looked forbidding, but
she wasn't intimidated. She knew him well enough to
know that he would never intentionally hurt her. But
weren't the unintentional hurts even worse?

She tried to imagine what his reaction would be if she
told him about the pregnancy. He would be shocked, but
then, when the shock had worn off, would come the
hasty retreat, the assurances of financial help, the excuse
about not being ready to settle down, the growing, in-
escapable fear that she might try and coerce him into a
situation he didn't want.

'Perhaps we could go into the sitting room,' and she

hurried out of the kitchen before he could refuse. It was bad enough having to deal with this, without having to do so perched on a hard kitchen chair.

She switched off the main overhead light and, instead, turned on two side lamps so that a mellow glow spread through the room. She curled up on one of the chairs, tucking her legs underneath her.

'There's something going on here, Sophie, some kind of hidden agenda, and I want to know what the hell it is.' He sat down and leaned forward, with his elbows resting on his knees, and he looked at her steadily.

'Hidden agenda?' Sophie laughed a little. 'I have no idea what you're talking about.'

'Is there someone else?' It was less of a question than a blunt demand, and she shook her head in bewilderment.

'Of course there isn't someone else!' she protested, hearing some anger in her voice as she absorbed his lack of faith in her. 'How could you even *think* that? Do you imagine that I've kept myself tucked away here for years, and then suddenly I've been overwhelmed by the urge to sleep with as many men as I can?' The anger felt good. It distracted her from the misery and confusion for a little while. 'How dare you suggest such a thing!'

Gregory didn't say anything for a while. He just looked at her steadily, and then he sat back in his chair and crossed his legs. 'So, if there's no one else on the scene, why the sudden change of mind?' His voice was slow, speculative and thoughtful, the sort of voice guaranteed to throw her into a spin—which it did.

This was foolish, she knew, because, as Kat had said, she had maybe three months of free time before he found out about the pregnancy. It was hardly as though it could be kept from him for ever. But, try as she may, she just couldn't see her way to telling him. Not now. Not when she felt so vulnerable. She needed a little time to get her courage into place.

'I just feel…' Sophie said, thinking quickly because it was clear that he simply didn't believe a word she'd said—or, rather, perhaps he did believe it, but he needed an explanation. 'I just feel that perhaps a fling, after all this time, wasn't the right thing for me.'

'The alternative being…?' he asked coolly, and when she didn't immediately answer he continued relentlessly, 'To remain in your state of frozen limbo? Live your entire life for Jade, and when she flies the coop devote what remains of your life to charitable deeds?'

'There's nothing wrong with that…'

'There is, if you happen to be young, beautiful and vibrant.'

'So, in other words, young, beautiful and vibrant women are wasted unless they find themselves a husband and get married and settle down?' She could feel the tears trying to surface through the anger because the thought of what she would now never have was almost too unbearable to stand. 'You forget that I've tried all that!'

'Come and sit here next to me.'

Sophie tucked her hair behind her ears and looked at him. No, she couldn't possibly go and sit next to him, but how she wanted to! She wanted to curl into a ball and feel his arms around her. She wanted him to tell her that everything was going to be all right.

But this, she lectured herself firmly, was a reality, and in reality everything didn't always turn out to be all right. In fact, they seldom did.

What if she told him about the baby? What would he say to comfort her? That a baby was just the thing he'd been hoping for? That he couldn't wait to dive, elbow-deep, into nappies and Babygros and sleepless nights?

That he was overjoyed at the prospect of relinquishing his freedom?

'I'd rather not.'

'Why? Because you might feel your willpower dissolving?'

Silence.

'Why aren't you talking to me?' he asked eventually. 'I'm trying to find out what the hell is going on here!'

'Why?'

'What?'

'Why are you trying to find out? Why is it so hard for you to accept?'

'Oh, for God's sake. I hope we're not going to return to those well-worn arguments about male pride.' He stared at her. 'Out of the blue you phone me up and say you want to talk. Then, hey presto! You inform me that you've changed your mind about us! No reason. Just a woman's prerogative!'

'I guess,' Sophie said, grappling with her words and trying to put them in such a way that they made sense without saying much in the process, 'I guess when I started…when I decided…well, I thought I could handle a fling, but I was wrong. I'm no spring chicken any more, and perhaps what I really want is commitment after all. Marriage, a wedding ring, commitment. All those horrid little things I thought I could well do without because I'd left them all behind and good riddance.' Well, all that was true.

'I imagined, stupidly, that Alan had inured me against another long-term relationship. I thought that the only thing I needed was something light and frothy. For the past few years just the thought of getting too close to someone had always been enough to make me lock myself a little tighter in my ivory tower. I couldn't contemplate going through all those feelings again…the hurt, the vulnerability. I simply assumed that when it came to men the one thing I didn't want was involvement. I knew what involvement entailed and I wanted no part of it.'

She sighed. 'I was wrong. What I find I need is to belong, to fit into someone else's life and let him fit into mine. Boring, isn't it? So much for your cherished ideas about my strength. I want to be married and to settle down. At last.'

Stepping so close to what was in her heart made her feel heady. What would he do, she wondered, if she just left it there? If she placed the ball in his court and waited to see what he would do with it? It was a gamble she wasn't about to take. She couldn't live with the appalled expression she would see creep slowly across his face. 'Not with you, of course.'

A dark flush crept into his cheeks, but for a long time he didn't say a word and the silence was so profound that she could almost hear it. Every small sound became magnified until the silence was almost a din.

'Of course not,' he said heavily. He stood up and eyed her coldly. 'Well, I guess there's not much more to be said, is there?' He barely bothered to glance in her direction as he strode towards the door of the sitting room. Now that he was actually on his way out, out of the front door, out of her house, out of her life—Sophie felt an insane desire to keep him here, even if it meant going round and round the same old arguments. Just so that she could have a few more precious moments of seeing his face, hearing his voice.

Was this what it felt like to be in love? This sharp, ripping pain at the thought of never feeling him touch her again? Or seeing the way his eyes crinkled when he laughed? She'd never felt that way with Alan.

Gregory got his coat, slung it on and then turned to look at her. His eyes were cool.

'I'd advise you to take a good, long, hard look at what you want out of life, Sophie, because, from where I'm standing, I don't think you have a clue. What's it to be next week? Still yearning for commitment or hankering after the casual fling?'

'You'd be surprised how much of a clue I have,' she answered truthfully, meeting his direct gaze without flinching. 'I know exactly what I want for the first time in my life.'

'And exactly what you don't want.'

She looked down when he said this, and he turned abruptly on his heel and walked towards the front door, opening it and then slamming it behind him without looking back.

It was only a little after ten. It had taken a little over two hours to just about stomach a meal, conduct the most difficult conversation she would ever have to conduct in her entire life and put paid to any dreams she might have had for happiness.

She collapsed onto her bed and let the thoughts revolve in her head, allowing herself the maudlin indulgence of dwelling on a future of pain and loss.

Over the next two weeks a strange feeling of unreality persisted. To go from a state of complete, satisfied happiness to one of total misery was almost too much to absorb.

After wondering what she should do about the pregnancy—whether she should go and register at her doctor, what precisely the etiquette was for someone who was newly pregnant—she decided to do nothing. She had no morning sickness, no symptoms at all, and she was perfectly happy to drift along, brooding on her problems, and let the pregnancy take its course, at least until she was three months pregnant. It had been a while since she'd had Jade, but she knew that she couldn't feasibly postpone a visit to her doctor much after that.

There was so much that she would have to deal with once she began to show that her mind seemed unable, or unwilling, to take it all in, at least just at the moment.

Aside from Jade and Gregory, she thought wryly, in this little drama there would be the clucking noises made by everyone who knew her in the village.

In the meantime, she meandered along in a daze, half hoping to accidentally bump into Gregory, half hoping that she wouldn't.

'You can't hide away for ever,' Kat told her over lunch one day, and Sophie nodded glumly.

'I know.'

'There's Jade, for a start. You'll have to explain it to her.'

'I know.' Sophie sipped her tea, eyed the remainder of her cheese and smoked ham sandwich with distaste and sighed. 'Not to mention Gregory, followed by the entire population of Ashdown. Honestly, Kat, if it weren't for Jade I would be seriously tempted to do a runner. Hibernate somewhere very far away.'

'No, you wouldn't. You're stronger than you think.'

'*Was*. I *was* strong, or so I thought. Really, I was just waiting in the wings for my turn to get on stage and reveal my true colours.' She pushed the plate to one side and cupped her chin thoughtfully in the palm of her hand.

Poor old Kat, she thought, bombarded by every nuance of emotion she, Sophie, had felt ever since she'd discovered the pregnancy. It was as if her feelings were too big to be contained. It made her realise how relatively unscathed she had been by her experiences with Alan, even if they had seemed profoundly catastrophic at the time. She had certainly never felt any real, overwhelming temptation to bare her soul the way she did now.

She looked back at the way she'd picked up the pieces, tearfully but competently, and had carried on with her life, always convinced that she was doing absolutely the right thing. In retrospect, she admired herself and her handling of that situation, and she only wished that she could call upon a similar level of willpower and single-mindedness now. But it seemed that she couldn't. The bottom of her world appeared to have dropped out, and she couldn't even think of picking up the pieces without feeling ill.

'I still think—'

'I know,' Sophie interrupted. Kat had made her feelings on the subject patently clear. Sophie and Gregory, she had said repeatedly, needed to talk. Emotions needed to be discussed. Sophie, she insisted, could not simply assume that she knew everything there was to know about Gregory and how he would react under the circumstances. Sophie had given up trying to explain to her friend that she knew how Gregory would react—she just did.

She assumed, later that evening, when Kat called that she would inevitably have more of the same to say to her, and her mind was already beginning to drift when Kat said nervously, 'I hope you won't hate me, Soph…'

Sophie's brain went onto full alert. Something in that tone of voice warned her that the next sentence wasn't going to be one that she wanted to hear. 'Hate you for what?' she asked tentatively.

There was enough of a pause to make her wonder whether they had been cut off, and she was about to speak when Kat said, in a barely audible whisper, 'For telling Gregory about the pregnancy…'

'*For telling him what?*'

'He's on his way over now, Soph... I thought I'd better warn you...'

The line went dead.

Sophie stared at the telephone incredulously, then every nerve in her body seemed to go into overdrive as she waited for the doorbell to ring.

CHAPTER TEN

THIS was the very worst thing that Kat had ever done. It was, Sophie thought, as she prowled through the sitting room, feeling her stomach clench and unclench, treachery on a substantial scale.

She'd known that she would have had to face this confrontation sooner or later, but she had chosen to stick her head in the sand. Now that it was being forced out she didn't know if she could handle the situation.

What was she going to do? What was she going to say?

She paused by the window, peering out and seeing nothing but blackness, and forced herself to calm down.

In a way, she decided, Kat had done her a favour. True, she had wanted to put the whole thing off until the last possible minute, but at least if she faced it now the prospect of Gregory would be off her mind. She would no longer have to live with the foreboding of what was going to inevitably happen.

She heard his car on the drive, and swallowed deeply before she went to the front door and opened it before Gregory had time to ring the bell.

'Kat warned me that you were on your way,' she said, marvelling at how normal her voice sounded when everything inside her was a jumbled, chaotic mess.

She risked looking at his face and immediately wished she hadn't because the lines of fury she saw there made her want to run and hide under the nearest table.

'I am not going to say a word until we're both inside,' Gregory told her, pushing past her into the small hall.

'You should be relieved to hear that I am going to do my best to control my rage.' He removed his coat, slung it over the banister and turned to face her with his arms folded.

'I have no idea why you should be angry,' Sophie told him, folding her arms as well so that they now faced one another like combatants sizing each other up in preparation for a fight. 'This isn't your problem.' She spun on her heel and walked ahead of him into the sitting room, her head held high.

So, she thought, he was angry, was he?

She could feel him behind her, controlling his temper—at least for the moment. She sat on one of the chairs and tucked her legs underneath her. She had to resist a strong temptation to place her hands protectively on her stomach. Instead, she rested her arms on the sides of the chair and watched in silence as he sat on the sofa.

It took all her strength just to look at him. How could it be that in so short a space of time she had managed to accumulate such a huge bank of memories?

'So,' he said coldly, 'it's not my problem.' His voice, steady and unhurried, carried the force of a whiplash. 'And when, exactly, had you intended to tell me about the…situation?'

Sophie went red and hastily looked away. She could feel the pulse in her neck, beating hard. 'I wish you'd try and understand how I feel…' she said in a clear but slightly unsteady voice.

'And how *do* you feel?'

'That this wasn't part of the deal…'

'Deal?'

She looked at him and gripped the sides of the chair.

'This wasn't meant to happen,' she corrected herself, lowering her voice. 'None of this was meant to happen.' She felt genuine anguish as she said this because she meant it so sincerely. None of this had been meant to happen. She hadn't meant to meet this man and fall in love with him, she hadn't meant to find herself hurt and aching, and she certainly hadn't meant to find herself pregnant.

She took a few deep breaths to steady herself.

'But happen it has,' Gregory said cuttingly, and she felt tears spring to her eyes. This she remembered clearly from when she had been pregnant with Jade—the hormones so close to the surface, turning her into an emotional wreck.

She blinked them back, determined not to collapse, which was what she really felt like doing. She could control this situation if only she could get a grip on herself.

'Yes, I'm afraid it has. I was stupid...I miscalculated...' Her voice petered out and for a while she just stared at him, completely at a loss as to how to continued.

'Isn't that rather beside the point?'

'I realise that you must be angry with me.'

'Oh, you realise that, do you?' He made an impatient sound under his breath and raked his fingers through his hair. Sophie recognised the gesture as one of deep frustration, but what, she thought helplessly and a little angrily, did he expect her to do? Why couldn't he just appreciate that at least she wasn't going to drag him into anything he didn't want?

There were many men who would have breathed a sigh of relief that they weren't about to be thrust into premature fatherhood, that they were being freed from any undue responsibility. If she and Alan hadn't been married, and this had occurred, she knew that he would have left without a backward glance and a clear conscience.

'Look,' she said, standing and stretching her legs, then sitting again, 'I've thought about this, God knows, I've done nothing else but think about it since I found out, and I think I've been more than fair.'

'You think...*what*?' he exploded. He strode across to where she was sitting and leaned over her so that his face was thrust menacingly close to hers. Automatically she pressed herself back into the chair.

'Could you please, just...go back to where you were sitting?' Sophie asked, in the soothing voice of someone very alarmed, trying to pacify an unpredictable beast.

'No, I like it right here. Up close. In fact...' He paused then lifted her bodily from the chair and carried her, protesting, to the sofa, where he unceremoniously deposited her. He sat next to her, yanking her back when she made an attempt to leap off.

'In fact...this is much better. I want to be very near to you when you start your little explanation of how you planned on separating me from my offspring.'

'I didn't plan on doing any such thing!' Sophie denied heatedly.

'Oh, really? Convince me.' His voice was cool and level and threw her into a state of deepening panic. What did he want her to say?

'I planned on telling you... Of course I did...'

'Because you would have had no option?'

The accuracy of the remark brought a faint, guilty blush to her cheeks and she had to restrain herself from leaping into a long, self-justifying monologue.

'I suppose that figured in it,' Sophie told him truthfully, and his brows met in a thunderous frown.

'When I met you,' she said, ploughing on in the face of his rising anger, 'I had no idea that I would end up sleeping with you.' If memory served her right, she thought bitterly, she'd been openly dismissive about the man before she'd even set eyes on him. 'But it happened. If it had been allowed to carry on in the natural course of things it would have fizzled out—we both know that. The fact that I'm now pregnant doesn't change that fact.'

'It damn well does change it,' Gregory told her icily.

'I don't see how,' Sophie persisted. She leaned forward in an attempt to communicate her message to him, and drew back when she realised that her shirt was gaping open at the front, revealing a great deal more than it concealed. 'This was only ever meant to be a casual fling!'

Casual fling. What a nice ring that had to it. As if it had ever been that for her.

'So what do you suggest, Sophie? That I bow out politely? Move house perhaps so that I can make your life a little easier?'

'Is that so bad? Most men would jump at the chance.'

'We're back to your ex-husband, I take it?'

'That has nothing to do with…this.'

'And what if I don't intend to bow out gracefully?'

She felt a sudden flare of panic at what those words conveyed, and swallowed it.

'Can we discuss this like two adults?' she said in a pleading voice. 'I know it must be a terrific shock to you, but I don't want to drag you into anything…drag us both into anything. I agree that it affects you…'

'How broad-minded of you!' he said scathingly. 'So now that we're discussing it like *two adults*, what's your proposal? You throw me a few visiting rights? Every other Sunday, perhaps?'

Sophie didn't say anything. She'd thought about what would happen once the baby was born, but had resolutely decided that it was simply a bridge she would cross when the time came. Now he was thrusting the decision onto her shoulders and her mind found it difficult to grapple with the potential problem.

'And every so often I slip something into the kitty to make sure my child doesn't go without?'

'Well, what do *you* suggest?' she flared. 'I'm merely trying to be sensible about the whole thing. It's not your fault that I'm pregnant...' That made no sense whatsoever, and she amended hastily, 'I mean, I thought that I was in a safe period at the time, and unfortunately I wasn't. I'm not about to punish you for my misjudgment. The fact is, like I said, neither of us wanted anything like commitment out of our relationship and I appreciate that.' She was running out of steam.

'I wondered why you suddenly decided to hijack the relationship,' he said in a cold, musing voice. 'Were you so terrified that I might suggest something more permanent if I found out about the pregnancy?'

'No,' Sophie said, surprised at that line of thought. 'It never crossed my mind, to be honest. I just thought that—'

'That you had to get away from me?'

'You're putting words into my mouth!' She wished that he hadn't dragged her over to this sofa. It was intimidating to be this close to him, wanting to touch him, knowing that was now the last thing she could possibly do. 'I'm just trying to deal with this—'

'In a sensible manner. I know, you said. Well, I have no intention of being sensible about this. You're carrying *my* child—'

'*Our* child,' she corrected him.

He looked at her carefully and for an awkwardly long time, without saying anything. 'I think the best course of action would be for us to get married.'

'What? Are you crazy?' *Get married?* It was the one thing she desperately wanted, but not like this. Not under these circumstances. A marriage of convenience to a man who wanted to do the right thing for the sake of a child he had fathered unknowingly.

'It makes perfect sense.'

'It makes no sense *whatsoever*. You seem to forget that I've already had my share of bad marriages. Do you honestly imagine that I'm going to launch myself into another one?'

He flushed darkly and looked away. 'I'm not proposing that you launch yourself into a bad marriage,' he said abruptly. 'Why do you necessarily assume that it would be *bad*?'

'Because it takes more than good sex to make a good marriage,' Sophie told him roughly. 'Marriage isn't a business deal.'

'But sleeping with me was,' he pointed out.

'Stop trying to run circles around me!'

'Do you hate me?' he asked, staring away from her. 'Is that it?'

'Of course I don't hate you.' She could feel a fine prickle of perspiration breaking out.

'Then…what?'

'Then…nothing.' She looked at him despairingly and he held her gaze.

'I realize that marriage is more than just good sex, as you put it, but isn't that a start?'

'You don't have to do this, Gregory. You don't have to volunteer for something you had no intention of getting into just because I'm pregnant.'

'I know.'

'You know?' Her head felt as though it were stuffed with cotton wool. Nothing was making sense, least of all the expression on his face, which she couldn't fathom. Not cold, not unsympathetic, just a certain awkwardness which only served to increase her sense of utter confusion. 'Then why…?'

'Two parents are better, surely, than one…'

'I'm not going to stop you from seeing your child. I thought that I'd made that perfectly clear.'

'Also…'

It was her turn to stare at him to try and understand what it was he was trying to say, but for the life of her she couldn't.

'Also,' he said, looking at her challengingly, 'I happen to think that…'

'That…?' she prompted, totally bewildered.

'I don't see any reason why…what I'm trying to say is…frankly, I'm not dismayed by this pregnancy. Obviously I'm a little shocked, yes, simply because it's unexpected, but, no, I can't say that I'm dismayed by this turn of events.'

'You're not?'

'I happen to think…' He stopped, as though unable to find the necessary words to continue.

She waited for him to finish, and as the silence lengthened between them she said eventually, 'You happen to think…what?'

'Why do you imagine that it would be a disaster, being married to me? I'm house-trained in all the essential areas…' Gregory gave her a look which was half glaring, half defiant, and made her heart flip over several times. 'I think you could grow to like me. You might even grow to love me, Sophie.' His voice dropped as he'd said this.

'Love…?' she said, amazed. How had that little word suddenly cropped up in the conversation?

'I realise that permanence didn't feature in your grand master plan. You complain bitterly about your ex-husband but, as far as I know, he might have been the great love of your life and you feel incapable of reproducing the feeling, without taking the risk of being hurt again.'

'*The great love of my life?*' She laughed bitterly. 'Oh, no. You've got it all wrong there, I assure you. When I look back on Alan love is the last thing that springs to mind. Youthful infatuation, perhaps. A lot of naïvete. But not love. No, love is…'

'Love is what?'

'Not that,' Sophie answered abruptly. 'It's also not something that you learn just because you happen to be in a certain situation. You don't love me, Gregory,' she said gently, 'and you never will. I was a challenge to you and now things have got a little out of hand, but don't kid yourself that marrying me is going to turn a challenge into something more.'

'Listen to me, Sophie. And don't interrupt. OK? I freely admit that I was attracted to you from the first minute I laid eyes on you, and I freely admit that, yes, you were initially a challenge. I had never met anyone like you before. You had all these walls around you and I wanted to be the one to chip away at them.' He scowled at her, daring her to say something, but she maintained a stunned silence, not quite knowing where all this was leading and curious to determine the destination.

'No doubt you think that that's a typically male, chauvinistic attitude, but you laid down your ground rules from the word go, and I just assumed that all was fair in love and war. There was a powerful attraction between us and I was more than willing to play the rules of your game.'

Sophie felt that she was fast losing the ability to think clearly. There was an excitement stirring deep inside her, making her giddy, and she licked her lips nervously.

'I'm no innocent when it comes to the opposite sex. I was sure that I could handle whatever situation arose.' He paused and looked away from her. 'I was wrong,' he muttered under his breath, and Sophie gave a sharp, painful inhalation. She could hardly believe what she was hearing. She was sure that she was missing some vital point, somehow misinterpreting his words and turning them into something that bore no relation to the truth. She fought to control a spreading excitement.

Gregory glanced sideways at her. 'Somewhere along the line something changed. It stopped being a situation I could handle. I went from wanting you to needing you…and then…well, I've never said this to any woman in my life before, never even been tempted to…but the fact of the matter is…I'm sure you know what I mean…I'm certain you don't need me to put it into words…just enough to say that marrying you…' He gave up completely and glared at her accusingly.

A slow smile spread across her face, a smile that started somewhere inside, before manifesting itself on the outside, a smile of pure, unadulterated bliss. Even if she'd misread every single thing, just to feel this happy was worth it.

'Yes,' he told her, watching her face, 'it's all very amusing, isn't it?'

'No.' She looked at him from under her lashes. 'Amusing isn't the word I'd use. I wish you'd just come right out and say what you have to say, though.'

'Well, why not? In for a penny, in for a pound, as they say. I've fallen in love with you. When, where and how this happened I have no idea, but it's happened and I'm personally overjoyed that you're pregnant. I'm afraid that I have no qualms about being absolutely selfish. I'm more than prepared to drag you, kicking and screaming, to an altar, and, so help me, God, I won't rest until I've turned whatever fleeting attraction you have for me into something deeper. There, I've said it. I thought I'd break down your walls, Sophie, but in the end you broke down walls I never knew I had. So how does it feel? You played your game and ended up with quite a few things you hadn't banked on.'

'How does it feel?' For a second she closed her eyes and breathed deeply. 'It feels absolutely…wonderful…' When she looked at him again her eyes were ablaze with emotion she had spent so long trying to suppress. 'No, better than wonderful.' She sighed. Alarmingly, she wanted to burst into tears and she blinked rapidly.

'Say that again,' he murmured, huskily, drawing her close to him, against his chest, where she could hear the steady hammering of his heart. 'Over and over. Tell me that you love me…'

'I do. You're the first I've ever loved.' She rested the flat of her hand against his chest and allowed herself to succumb to the heady satisfaction of contentment. 'And I only realised how much when I discovered that I was carrying our child. I felt like someone who'd stupidly but deliberately made their way down a very deep hole, and realised how impossible escape was when they looked up and could no longer see the light.'

She tilted her face to his and made a small, purring sound as his lips covered hers, a deep, warm, gloriously fulfilling kiss that carried the promise of eternity.

His hand, resting on her neck, moved to touch her still flat stomach, then slipped underneath her shirt to caress her breast, already fuller with the pregnancy. She felt its heavy weight in his hand and sat up straighter, bending back and moaning lightly as his hand continued to stroke and massage and tease her engorged nipple.

'So, are you saying that you'll marry me?' His breath in her ear was warm and stirring.

'I feel I have no choice.' She grinned and undid the buttons of his shirt, pushing her hands against his chest then up to his collarbone. 'I'm not showing yet so there's still time for us to enjoy…well, you said it, good sex. Very good sex.'

She stripped off her shirt and lifted one breast to him so that he could take the swollen nipple in his mouth, which he did, sucking on it as she curled her fingers in his dark hair, her body working itself up to a peak of pleasure.

'And just wait until you do start to show, my witch. Sex, I assure you, will never be so good.' He rolled his fingers along the peak of her nipple and then angled her down so that he could explore her mounting wetness through her lacy briefs. 'I happen to find pregnancy a very arousing condition.'

'Just so long as it's *this* pregnant woman you have in mind,' Sophie whispered, feeling ready to cry again.

'Oh, yes. I guess that's what this love thing is all about. My love.'

EPILOGUE

IT HAD felt strange to go through the marriage vows again, with a baby on the way and Jade, deliriously happy to be a bridesmaid, painstakingly making sure that she didn't put a foot wrong.

Sophie had worn cream because, as she'd explained to Gregory, it *was* the second time around for her.

'But not for me,' he had told her, grinning, 'so do you mind if I wear white?'

'Go right ahead,' she had teased, 'but I should skip the veil if I were you. It might not suit you.'

He had worn black, and when she'd raised her eyes to his the sight had filled her with such emotion that she'd had to look away or risk bursting into tears.

Which wouldn't have been such a good idea, considering the turn-out of people to wish them well—a steady stream which had begun early in the morning and continued through the day. Most of the village had come, it seemed, all disproportionately pleased at the surprising turn of events. They had welcomed Gregory with open arms from the start, and were delighted that he'd taken the irrevocable step that would root him firmly in their community.

Sophie would never have believed that pregnancy could have been such a joyous experience—the gentle swell, the first kick, then growing bigger. How different from the last time when her changing body had turned her into a pariah. The memory, once so painful, was nothing more than a distant blur, a reminder of a past that she had finally and joyfully shed.

Now, relaxing in the deep, comfortable sofa in the sitting room, with the darkness outside pressing against the windowpanes, she looked at her family and felt her heart flip with love and pride.

'A boy!' Gregory had told her exultantly, seconds after the baby had been born. 'I fear you might well find yourself in the company of two builders.'

Their son was a little over a week old now and held an apparently bottomless fascination for Jade and Gregory. They couldn't believe how *small* he was. Jade was consumed with awe at the thought that she, too, had once been that tiny.

Sophie looked across at her husband on the sofa next to her, and watched as he arranged Jade next to him and then scooped the baby out of the Moses basket, carefully positioning him in her lap.

He looked up, caught her eye and grinned.

'It must be like having her very own doll,' he said over Jade's head, extending his arm along the back of sofa and linking his fingers with Sophie's.

Sophie smiled back at him wryly. 'That's because she's fast asleep when he wakes up during the night, demanding a feed. And, to be honest, he *is* a contented little soul.'

'Isn't he, though?' Gregory said comfortably. 'Takes after me in that respect.'

'I notice that fatherhood hasn't done much to curb that modest streak of yours.'

'Well, I *am* rather proud of the little lad.' The 'little lad' had been called James after Sophie's father and Thomas after Gregory's grandfather. Gregory stroked her thumb with his finger and she felt that amazing stirring of her senses, which she experienced every time he touched her.

She ran her fingers through Jade's hair. She looked

up and smiled, then mouthed, 'Can I walk round the room with him?'

'Absolutely not!' Sophie said, laughing. Speaking very slowly and clearly, she said, 'You're still just a baby yourself!'

'Tomorrow we'll go for a walk and you can push the pram,' Gregory said, tilting Jade's face to his so that she could read his lips, and she smiled with enthusiasm. 'Right now, though, it's bed for you.' Upon which he gently levered the baby out of her arms and cradled him, smiling as he stirred in his sleep, dreaming baby thoughts, reaching up with closed fists. Then he transferred the baby carefully back into the basket and sat close to Sophie, stroking her hair and then making a face as his fingers tangled in the red, curling mass.

'Some things change,' she said, laughing, 'but unfortunately my hair isn't going to be one of them.'

'Good.' He traced the contours of her face with his fingers. 'Hang onto that hair of yours. When I start balding we can lop some of it off and turn it into a toupee for me.'

'Oh, very fetching.'

She kissed him on the lips, a light, sensuous kiss, then drew back to look at him.

'Isn't this perfect?' he murmured, and she felt his breath against her hair. 'Isn't this paradise?'

'Yes. Yes, it is. Who would have thought that I would have ended up marrying the man who walked into the library all those months ago, demanding a book about the village?'

'Demanding? Me?' He nuzzled her ear. 'You bewitched me, and now you're stuck with me for life.'

'I think I can cope with that.' She glanced at the baby, asleep with his arms outstretched by his head. 'I think I can cope with paradise.'

The world's bestselling romance series.

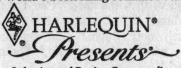

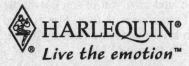

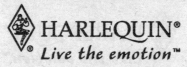

The world's bestselling romance series.

HARLEQUIN®
Presents

Seduction and Passion Guaranteed!

A gripping, sexy new trilogy from

Miranda Lee

THREE RICH MEN...

Three Australian billionaires—they can have anything, anyone...except three beautiful women....

Meet Charles, Rico and Ali, three incredibly wealthy friends all living in Sydney, Australia. Up until now, no single woman has ever managed to pin down the elusive, exclusive and eminently eligible bachelors. But that's about to change, when they fall for three gorgeous girls....

But will these three rich men marry for love— or are they desired for their money...?

Find out in Harlequin Presents®

A RICH MAN'S REVENGE—Charles's story
#2349 October 2003

MISTRESS FOR A MONTH—Rico's story
#2361 December 2003

SOLD TO THE SHEIKH—Ali's story
#2374 February 2004

Available wherever Harlequin® books are sold

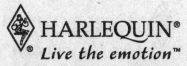

HARLEQUIN®
Live the emotion™

Visit us at www.eHarlequin.com

HSR3RM2

National Bestselling Author

brenda novak

COLD FEET

Despite the cloud of suspicion that followed her father to his grave, Madison Lieberman maintained his innocence...*until* crime writer Caleb Trovato forces her to confront the past once again.

"Readers will quickly be drawn into this well-written, multi-faceted story that is an engrossing, compelling read."
—*Library Journal*

Available February 2004.

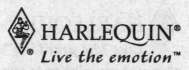

HARLEQUIN®
Live the emotion™

Visit us at www.eHarlequin.com

PHCF

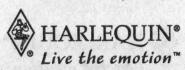

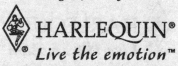

The world's bestselling romance series.

HARLEQUIN®
Presents

Seduction and Passion Guaranteed!

GREEK TYCOONS

They're the men who have
everything—except a bride…

Wealth, power, charm—what else could
a heart-stoppingly handsome tycoon need?
In the GREEK TYCOONS miniseries you have
already been introduced to some gorgeous
Greek multimillionaires who are in need of wives.

THE GREEK TYCOON'S SECRET CHILD
by Cathy Williams
on sale now, #2376

THE GREEK'S VIRGIN BRIDE
by Julia James
on sale March, #2383

THE MISTRESS PURCHASE
by Penny Jordan
on sale April, #2386

**Pick up a Harlequin Presents® novel and you will
enter a world of spine-tingling passion and
provocative, tantalizing romance!**

Available wherever Harlequin books are sold.

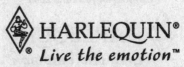

HARLEQUIN®
Live the emotion™

Visit us at www.eHarlequin.com

HPGT2004